WHEN GODS
FAIL

■

RESURRECTION

NELSON LOWHIM

Also By Nelson Lowhim

The Struggle Trilogy

CityMuse

Tree of Freedom

Ministry of Bombs

Alternative Book Press
2 Timber Lane
Suite 301
Marlboro, NJ 07746
www.alternativebookpress.com

2014 Paperback Edition
Copyright 2014 © Nelson Lowhim
Cover Illustration by Nelson Lowhim
Book Design by Nelson Lowhim
All rights reserved
Published in the United States of America by Alternative Book Press

Originally published in electronic form in the United States by Eiso Publishing.
Library of Congress Cataloging-in-Publication Data

Nelson, Lowhim, [date]
When Gods Fail III/ by Nelson, Lowhim.—1st ed.
p. cm.
1. Science—Fiction (Fiction). I Title.
PN1-6790-380.L69W446   2013
813'.6—dc23
2014903959

ISBN 978-1-940122-10-6
Printed in the United States of America
10 9 8 7 6 5 4 3 2 1

"...cursed be he that keepeth back his sword from blood" — Jeremiah 48:10

I walk outside and see John staring at me. There are guards beside him. They're grim.

"I got him. The traitor disgusted me too much." I stare John right in the eyes. For a moment I think of wavering, of looking away, and there's even some fear. But I remind myself of all that I'd done, the people I'd killed, and I keep staring. Try to grab his eyes with my stare and twist him down. It works. He glances over at the door.

"You shot him?" he asks.

"He was a liar," I say, hoping that the part of me that trembles for what I've done doesn't surface. Don't show them weakness. Never beg.

The soldiers and guards look to John. They're agitated, and I can sense that it's me that they want in that chair.

John breaks a smile. It's one that only cracks the side of his lips; his eyes are stone cold. "I couldn't stand him myself," he says.

I nod my head and force a smile. "I know. Bastard had us all fooled," I say. I feel nauseous and try to stifle the rumbles coming from my gut. There's a weakness forming in my legs. I need to stop it before they sense it. I take a deep breath, glancing over at all of them, then back to John.

John turns to the other men. "Clean everything up and burn his body." The men hesitate, some glare at me. I make sure to glare back. Blood rushes to my head and fists.

The men go inside. They grumble. Some of them kick the body. I try to focus on something else.

John steps up to me, places a hand on my shoulder. I'm grateful for what he's done, for showing some flexibility with me.

"You sure you're all right?" he asks.

"Of course," I say. "Why wouldn't I be?"

He stares into me. I'm not certain if he's trying to intimidate me, or if he's just looking for the truth. Either way, I make sure to lock into his eyes.

"You really didn't like him, did you?" he says more so than asks.

"He was a friend," I say, making sure to emphasize the was. "I trusted him, and he betrayed me. How would you feel after something like that?" I stare so hard into his pupils that I can see the reflection of the men lifting MacGee's body off the chair. One spits on it, and they all laugh. It takes more energy not to glance at them. Not to shoot them.

"I would do the same," John says. He sighs.

"Exactly," I say and step away from him. Part of me can't believe he's accepted this as a reasonable excuse, and part of me is jumping with joy that I was able to pull it off.

John's eyes dart over to the men as they carry out MacGee's body. I take a moment to do the same. MacGee hangs lifeless, carried on a stretcher. He somehow seems older and smaller than ever. His eyes are open, as is his mouth. I take deep breaths looking at him. I make certain that everyone sees me smile.

John places his arm around my shoulder. "Come talk with me," he says.

I follow him, somewhat glad to be away from those men who still seem to be eyeing me. We enter John's house. He closes the door and walks past me before I can say anything. Something starts to form in my chest. My eyes check every crevice to make sure there's no one else.

There's an aroma emitting from me, it's sour, like decay. I hope that John can't smell it. And what if he does? He did save my ass back there with those men. And though having killed MacGee makes me feel like crawling further and further inside my own head, body, I feel the awakening of the man who did all those horrible things so long ago. Or the creature that I'd been. It opens an eye, it unfurls it wings and my chest fills with it. Why should I care if John's men had said anything? None of them have been through what I have.

But Jenny. But MacGee. The only friend you ever had.

I grit my teeth. Be strong. John will sense the weakness.

"How's it going?" I ask.

John turns and looks me over.

"Why did you kill him? Were you trying to spare him the torture?"

As his face crunches up into a frown, I know I can't think for too long or else he'll know that I'm scheming. "Of course not," I say. There's no way I can let him know I have or had a weakness. I can't trust anyone with that anymore. I had MacGee for that, a man to trust with the worries of my mind, and I couldn't save him.

"No? Why then?"

"I told you, he disgusted me," I say.

John tilts his head and raises his eyebrows. "Come on, now. Let's not play around, Tom. I know that wasn't the reason." His hands sweep to the room around us. "We're alone, look for yourself. Just you and me." He pauses and looks me over, then scans the room himself as if to make sure no one has sneaked in. "Tell me what happened."

He's using a calm voice, and in his eyes I see a softness, something almost pleading. My hard stance melts. I force myself to think of MacGee. Of what John did to those men in the cave. The other Tom. John used me there. But he wants me as a friend, doesn't he? And how can I judge him? Does not the Bible say Judge not yest ye be judged? I'd done much worse than that. I killed an entire family. I was the reason Jenny died. My heart softens. "John," I say and that beast inside me growls. Don't be a fool. Whatever you've done is in the past. This is about surviving the now. And the softer side of me, the one piece of my brain that wants forgiveness for what I did to Jenny, MacGee, speaks up again: and what if John is that friend who will be able to hear out your problems? Will you throw that away too?

"Yes?" John asks. He seems slightly perturbed that I'm taking so long to answer his questions. He sounds concerned.

"I went into that shack to ask him a few questions."

"Why did you kick everyone out? We're all brothers. You should've been able to ask those questions in front of them," John says.

I'm sure I hear a certain amount of concern in the fricatives of his voice. "Why? Was that wrong?" I realize that I might not last the night.

"Yes," John says, very matter-of-fact like. "It was wrong." He waves his hand. "But don't worry about that. Just tell me why you did what you did. Tell me the truth."

And I'm glad that he has turned authoritative. My heart hardens. I know that I need to say whatever it is he wants to hear. Show weakness, but only enough to make it believable. "I wanted the truth from him. Why he attacked you. Why he would betray us all. When I was with him in the cave, he was brave," I say, thinking of how to make MacGee's change seem like a surprise. "I'd no idea he'd try to hurt you."

It takes all of my strength to stare John in the eye, to make sure that my voice doesn't crack, or give away the tension in my mind.

"I didn't know exactly what to expect when I was going to talk to him, so I decided to do it alone. He was my friend. A good friend, so what he did was exceptionally horrid," I say.

As I speak, I know my face's calm. One eye twitches. I narrow my eyes to prevent it from happening again. The neural pathways in my mind spark like live wires, trying to find the right words.

"If he was going to spit in my face, I wanted it man to man," I continue. "I didn't want his fear of the others to cloud his words." I take in a deep breath to calm myself down, to prevent my tongue from tripping over these words. "He admitted to wanting to destroy us all. When he said that, I knew that I'd been fooled." My eyes fall to the ground. I try to appear humbled, and I hope that John has taken the gambit. I look up. "So there you have it. He fooled me. You expect me to let him go on living?"

John eyes feel my face, then dart around the room. I follow his eyes to make sure there're no surprises.

He starts to nod. My feet itch to move.

"I suppose I would've done the same thing if someone close to me ever decided to betray me," John says, his voice low.

My heart jumps. Does he mean me? Do I even want that? I try to see if his face will tell what his words failed to say. He has a stone face-mask on, and his eyes have me locked in a vice grip. What can I read into that?

I decide to move my feet towards him. "Of course." I hear myself say. "One can never be too careful. But I think I speak for both of us when I say that you're one of the people in this group who I trust. And if there's someone you don't trust, we should keep an eye on him. Perhaps figure out a system to tell these people from the rest of us," I say and now I'm only a few feet away from him. I can smell his sweat, and I can see one bead of sweat roll down his forehead.

"I agree," he says. If he's sweating because of nervousness, his calm voice doesn't give him away.

I pause, wondering if I should ask him if he's talking about me betraying him. Or if he already considers this done. "I'm glad," I say. Perhaps this is better left unsaid. If I mention it he will have the idea planted in his head and it might work against me. But I also want to make sure that when I leave his place I won't be looking over my shoulder. I have to clear myself, in his mind at the least. The beast in me is growling. My hand reaches up and rests on his shoulder. I see him twitch.

"John. You believe me, don't you? MacGee," I say and steel myself for what I have to say next. "That cowardly bastard cut me deep. He tried to hurt you. To stop our progress. All this," I say and wave my free hand about. "Is for a reason, right?" I say and stare straight into his eyes. My heart pushes blood into my head. I think crystal thoughts. I need to make sure that he's not just listening to me, and participating in his own conversion to my side.

"You're right," he says, his eyes flick off mine for a second. He sounds like he's been caught off guard.

"We will create something new, and we will tear down anyone who comes between," I say. I wonder how this all sounds to him. It was me who asked for a trial for MacGee. That was before I knew he'd be tortured.

"We will." John maintains my stare.

We lock eyes for a few seconds. The rest of the room grows dark. I feel the air pressure increasing. I feel my chest bursting at the seams. What will I do next?

"Then, that's it, isn't it?" I say.

"It is."

"I'll see you tomorrow?"

"Yes," he says. "We'll have to explain why you killed MacGee before the trial."

I don't know what to make of this.

He breaks a half smile, but I know it's forced. I smile as well.

I move forward and embrace him. "How about a prayer?"

He cocks his head. "A prayer?"

"Of course. After all, it's been a busy few days. I think we have really grown as a kingdom. Don't you?" I say and pat his back, trying to give him the idea that I mean him. But I can't say it. Can't bring myself to kiss his ass.

"Of course."

I kneel, and he slowly follows suit. I bow my head and peak out of the corner of my eye to see that he's done the same thing. And he closes his eyes. I feel a brief moment of glee, as my balls push a hormone up to my chest, and I feel my teeth grit and my fists clench. That beast, that monster inside of me roars. Break his neck. He's not looking, end him. He's the one who killed your friend, MacGee. Do it.

I do not. I'm not even sure why. I close my eyes and say the Lord's Prayer. As I speak the words I can hear John mumble along with me. I try to feel a connection with him. Everything in me wants to know the same connectedness that I'd felt with Jame's family only a short while ago. But I don't. When I finish and we embrace again, and I walk outside.

Above the stars shine as bright as moons. Slowly the tension inside my chest and balls unwinds. I take in a deep breath and I can smell burning meat. I try not to think that it's MacGee's body burning, or just burned. Soon, I think to myself. But you can't just kill John. The problem isn't just him. Then what? I look over my back as if people are able to hear what's in my head. Sleepiness takes over, and I feel like heading back to my place.

I can't. The look of disrespect that those men had flashed me keeps me thinking. I can't hide. That's what they want. I haven't survived this long by hiding, have I? Just remember what being nice gets you. Pulling out my handgun, I check to make sure it's filled with bullets. I walk back to the place I shot MacGee.

The same men are standing around with brooms and mops in their hands. A low gruff mumbling reaches me. I cough and they start up. I see them all face me. There's that lightness in the air that indicates they've been talking about me. Remember that they're weaker than you. "How's it going?" I ask.

They glance at each other. Some take steps towards me.

"Have you cleaned out the room?" I ask. If I act even the least bit nice, they'll sense weakness. "Huh?" I ask louder. I see a couple of them flinch, but most of them sneer. Secretly, I want to turn to see if there's someone behind me. One word from John, and I'll be scrambling for my life. There's nothing to do now but charge forward.

"I asked a question," I say stepping forward. I see some of the men I've tussled with in the past. There's the man from the initial trial that the family, MacGee, and I had to suffer when we first came here. There's also the young man who tried to bully me the other night. These two are looking at me the hardest.

"No one wants to answer?" I say, step forward, and the man from the trial sneers at me harder. He has two friends to either side of him and none of them has a gun out.

I point at him. "You're not going to answer either?"

He puffs out his chest for a second, but as I try to literally grab his eyes with my stare, he backs off. I swing my torso forward and grab his collar. It rips. I pull him close to me. I don't want to escalate this into a full on fight, not right now. To my surprise, he stares me right in my eye. His breath smells like old eggs. I snarl at him.

"I asked a question, didn't I?" I can hear a couple others shuffle their feet. It's sporadic noise; which means they're looking at each other, confused.

"What?" he says, trying to stand up straight.

But I'm too strong for him. I twist him once more, making sure it's into my leg, and he stumbles. I hold him. He's very light, but my muscles start to weaken.

"You heard me," I say.

He twists his neck to see his friends, but I shake him and his head whips back. I can hear a grinding noise. He reaches out for my face, and I shake my head and cock one hand back.

"You try anything stupid, and I'll show you up worse than at the trial. And this time, John won't help you. You get my drift?"

"Okay," he says, his hands moving up in the surrender fashion. "We cleaned out the room. You." He indicates at the room. "Can see for yourself."

I pull him up to me, straighten out his torso, and smile. "Thank you. That's all I was asking." I let go of him.

The rest of them seem sheepish now.

"Everything going well?" I ask. I need to temper things down or else these men will be my enemies. That's something I don't need right now.

Some men mumble something that sounds like "yessir", and some nod their heads. All avoid my eyes.

"You seem down," I say. "Why? This is a glorious time for us. We've fought and destroyed a powerful enemy of ours." My body is rejecting the very notion of having to say such things, not when these very men just cleaned up the blood of a good friend of mine. I make sure to cast my eyes over them. "You know that it's only going to be better for us. We'll find our enemies from before, and they'll bow before us and the Lord, or they'll suffer the fate of all those who ever fought the Lord." I pause. I'm trying to say this as loud as possible without the thought of MacGee causing my voice to crack.

"Am I right?" I ask.

The men look at me, and they seem to believe what I've said. Some of them nod vigorously. I pick out the man I'd just shook about and point to him. "Am I right?"

"You're right," he says. He doesn't sound certain.

14

"I know I am. We will soon be masters of the world. The entire world. Think on that." With one hand sweeping the skies above me, I smile at them. They appear to be agreeing with me. "Get some sleep tonight, gentlemen. There will be more work to do tomorrow."

They nod their heads and break off in twos and threes and dissolve into the darkness.

When all of them have left, I think about heading back to my place to be alone. But first I decide that I need to snoop around. Only a few lights flicker in the alleyways, and through the cracks of houses. I walk flat-footed as I find a dark alley and sit down in the shadow of a house that's bursting with light and muffled sounds. I lean my head on the wall.

"Come on, you know you have to get ready for school," says a woman.

"I don't want to," replies a little girl.

A sharp slap. The sharp silence of pressure follows.

"Do you have to be so hard on them?" the woman says.

"You saw what happened today. The past two days. We're going to get attacked again. And everyone has to show some discipline. Especially her," a man replies.

Somewhere near, a door swings open. "Hi there." It's a young man. I can't match the voice to a face, but it sounds familiar. I'm certain it's one of the men from the group I just dispersed.

"Did everything go well?" the man asks.

"Fine," the young man replies. There's some hesitation.

"What's the matter?"

"Nothing."

Crosstalk. Then silence. I move away after a few minutes, wondering if they can somehow sense my presence. At least nothing was said. As I creep down the alley and stay in the shadows, I hear more voices, all men, coming from somewhere outside. It sounds hushed, forced, and angry whispers.

Around the corner I see three men huddled in a dark corner. I backtrack, move to a parallel alley before creeping up on them.

"I'm telling you, he was too strong to fight off."

15

It sounds like the man I roughed up earlier.

A half chuckle. "You sure didn't try too hard. He threw you around like a rag doll."

"Screw you," the man replies. "I'll show you how strong I am."

Some rustling ensues.

"Take it easy," a lower and softer voice says as the rustling ceases. "Let's not wake everyone up."

"No one lives in these houses."

"Still, let's not go crazy. We have to keep low. Besides, he's right. Tom's strong. He did the same thing to me a few days ago."

My chest brims with pride. I recognize the voice. It's that bully I saw in the same alleyway a few days ago. I take a slow breath and crouch low in the shadows, just in case someone decides to walk up behind me.

"Why the hell didn't you guys swarm him when he grabbed me?"

"What the hell were we supposed to do? He is John's friend, isn't he?"

"I don't know."

"What do you mean? He's always around John. And he helped in that battle."

"I was there. He didn't do anything. It was all John."

"And John thanked him."

"I think he's pussy. He saved his friend by shooting him. You didn't see his face when he kicked us out. He was trying to act tough. When he saw his friend I saw how much of a coward he was."

"You always thought he was weak."

"So?"

"I'm just saying that one needs to take John into account."

"You saw how pissed John was, didn't you?"

"Yeah, but he invited him back to his place."

"And John's the one who said Tom helped out in the battle."

A round of murmurs pass from the three men. I think it's them agreeing.

"That still don't explain why ya'll didn't help me."

"You yourself said he's strong."

"Not more than all of us."

"Well, we don't know about the others. They might never help us."

"A couple of them sounded like they liked him."

A wind picks up, and I can't hear exactly what's said next, though my name pops up a few times. Then the men walk off. I lean around the corner and try to make out the other two men's profiles. It's hard to say. They seem more hunched than most men, but perhaps it's because they're whispering. I stand up and walk in the other direction.

Did those men want revenge? Or were they just airing out grievances? I try to remember what the eyes of the man I throttled looked like. Were they scared or only buying time? Either way I'll have to look over my shoulder. What else can I do to that man? He's been shown how strong I am. And yet none of them seemed sufficiently scared of me. They're right, if enough of them gang up on me, I won't stand much of a chance.

And there's the nagging thought that I'm only alive because of John. That I'll only be spared because of him. Should I have helped MacGee when he had tried to kill John? Would the rest have fought me after that? Or would they've fallen in line?

My feet speed up as I think about Genevine and that moment we spent, of her smell, of being inside her. She can put my mind at ease.

I step inside my house and see the Genevine and two other women—the women I think live here with me—talking in the kitchen. They stare at each other. Again, I'm certain I've been talked about.

"Hi," I say, looking down.

"Hi," they say in unison.

When I look back up, Genevine is the only one staring at me, while the other two lean away from her.

The two make some excuses to leave, and I smell their softness as they walk past me. I lock the door and take a few steps towards Genevine. I'm not certain what they were talking about, but whatever it is, it still hangs in the air in front of her.

"You doin' all right?" I ask as I stop a few feet from her. Her face borders on fear.

"I'm fine," she says, holding eye contact, before looking down at her hands, her feet.

I look over my shoulder and to the locked door. "Why did they leave? They live here, right?"

"They do. But I told them I wanted some time alone."

"With me?" I ask.

She doesn't answer.

"What were you talking about?"

Again she doesn't answer.

I take a deep breath. I feel that everyone is rising against me. But why? The only wrong I've done is mercy-kill MacGee. And surely she didn't know about that already? Perhaps John was already tilling the ground, whispering into ears so I'll be easy to remove.

I take a step forward and Genevine shrinks back. I step away. For a second her aloofness reminds me of Jenny. And for another second her face morphs into Jenny's and my heart crumples. With as much energy as I can muster, I push the feeling aside. I need to focus on the now. Jenny is past.

Then I remember how angry MacGee was, how everyone had whispered about him. That's what made it easy to take him out, wasn't it? The whispers were already there.

To survive I'll either have to face everyone down, or try to bring them to my side. In the end, none of these people have been through what I have, and none of them are going to take me away from this world.

"Are you scared of me?" I ask.

She shakes her head while pursing her lips.

"Then what is it?" This time I step forward and take her hand. She tries to shake me off, but I hold on. "You were talking about me. So tell me what it was," I say, talking in a quiet, but all bass voice.

Her eyes fall to her feet before finally looking up at me. "Mary, you know the bigger one?"

18

The two women who just left aren't exactly big, though you can see in their bone structure that they'll fill up if given the chance. "What about her?"

"She's… with one of the men on the council," she says.

The council. The men at the table during the trial. It seemed like even John had to bow to their wishes. And outside of a few group events, I've never seen them.

"And?"

She looks at me like I'm an alien. "That's why we're talking about you."

My brain jolts within its casing. "And what did she say?" I ask, talking slowly, hoping it covers my panic.

"Nothing. They were talking about what you did in the cave."

I relax. "How I'm a hero?"

She raises her eyebrows.

"And what do you think?" I ask.

"I think it's all games. Men will be men."

I scrutinize her hard face and feel her eyes smiling. I now know what it is I found in her arms the last time I was with her. With one hand reaching around her waist, I lean in to kiss her. She pushes me away.

"That doesn't mean I'm yours for the taking. It's against the rules, you know."

"What?"

"Sex outside of marriage."

"Really?" I ask. I'm not sure, but somewhere in my brain there's a memory of John hinting that this wasn't the case. "What's the punishment?"

"Death," she says with a straight face.

"Death?"

"Well, stockades for two single people," she says and indicates to me and her. "And death if one is married."

That hits me hard. It means that I'll have to keep my relationship with Samantha under the wraps.

"Do they know about us?" I ask.

"No," Genevine replies, though it's not convincing.

"What do you mean no? How come they left us alone?"

"I said you were courting me."

The courting rituals I've read don't include leaving someone alone. I feel a rush as her hand brushes across my crotch. I smile at her.

She leads me to my bed and I get on top, feeling like we're going to be able to fight off the whole world with our act. I push into her, but my mind sits on the words those men outside spoke, and my moment with John. And MacGee. Soon I can't push, and I pull my limp member out.

She taps it playfully. "Oh, that's a let down."

"Sorry," I say sheepishly, though some anger rises up out of me. "My mind's elsewhere."

She plays, pulls it for a second, before she gives up and rests her head on her hand, looking at me with her head tilted.

"What's your mind on?" she asks. "The council?"

"Could be," I say and look her over, look at the shadows of her face for a hint at her true feelings. Am I made to try and open up to the first person I see, or think I can trust? She could very well turn me in. "Could be…" I repeat.

She rolls her eyes. This is not the woman I remember from before.

"That's the game you're going to play?" she says and takes a second to cast a dismissive look at my cock.

I shrink. "Well…" Why am I being so shy? I should know by now that one must not hesitate. Not in this new world. Remember how you survived. And yet, if the woman in front of me reminds me of Jenny, in only a few actions, perhaps I should remember what drove the woman I loved over the edge. And what of Carol? And what of MacGee?

"What do you think about MacGee?" I ask after the room is filled with nothing but the beat of my heart and the taste of some chemical in my mouth.

"The old man who tried to kill John?" she asks.

"That's the one."

She throws her hand in the air. "What about him? He tried to kill our leader, and now he'll pay."

She seems not to care. Though the way she said "leader" almost sounded derisive. "He's already dead," I say. I make certain not to mention what I did. Should I spread the word? It might be better than having others form the story for me. But I'm still not ready to talk about it. My mind might implode if I mention what I did. Just thinking about it makes me shiver.

She scrutinizes me. In a flash I see the unimpressed glance Jenny gave me more than once.

"Is he a friend of yours?" she asks.

"Of course. We came together, didn't we?"

"That doesn't mean much. People change alliances all the time," she says.

I nod my head. "He was a friend of mine." I feel sick to my stomach.

"Oh," she says. Now her scrutiny increases, and she shifts herself so she's closer to me. This revelation seems to have increased my standing in her mind. I'm trying to think why.

The way she breathes, for the next few seconds of silence, captivates me. I find something gnawing its way from my blood and bones to my mind. I'm not certain what.

"But you were the hero at the battle, while he went over to the other side," she says.

"That's right." I hesitate to say something in his defense.

Her eyes dart from my mouth to my eyes, then between them. "There's something you're not telling me," she says.

She's smart. Intelligent. I won't be able to get much past her.

"There's a lot I'm not telling you," I say.

She doesn't react to this.

"How old are you?" I ask.

Still no reaction. If I'm to guess from the lack of wrinkles, smooth skin, and slightly pushed cheeks, I would say eighteen. Yet she acts as controlled as a thirty-year-old.

"You can't be older than twenty," I say.

21

"Is that what you want to talk about, my age?" she says, and fakes a yawn.

If I decide to lock horns with her, it's obvious that I'll lose. At least when it comes to brainpower. "No, I don't," I say.

More silence.

"What do you think of John?" I ask.

"John?" she asks and smiles. "He's not what he wants people to think," she says.

"Why's that?"

"He just isn't."

"What does he want people to think?"

"That he's Jesus. That he has control. But he's a man like anyone else."

There's a hint of anger in her voice. "And how would you know that?"

"He made a pass at me. Tried to get me to sleep with him. So much for Jesus."

"Well, no man's perfect."

"But he makes the rules like he is, and he holds us all to them," she says.

"And the council? Are they any good?"

"They're the same. Just as bad. All of them have somehow managed to get us to agree that there won't be any more voting. We used to vote all the time. Then they stopped that after the Fall."

"The bombs?" I say.

She glances me over. "Are you like John?" she asks.

"What do you mean?"

"You seem to be his right-hand man," she says, her voice accusing.

That's not a bad thing, I think. It seems to be one of the main things that saved me with those men.

"I'm there, but that doesn't mean I'm him," I say. "Does the council do whatever John tells them to?"

"Pretty much. Though who knows what goes on behind closed doors."

"They meet a lot?" I ask.

"Seem to," she replies.

I jerk my head when I hear something like wood creaking.

"It's the house next doors," she says. She takes my hand, nestling herself on my arm. She settles and her head presses down on an artery. My arm slowly goes numb, tingling my fingers. Pain. But I can hear and feel her breath on my neck and cheek. I let her be. I like her this close.

"I am. What have people been saying about me?" I ask.

"Besides the *hero* thing?" she says.

"Yes".

"Nothing. A lot of them seem to like you."

"And the men?"

"Same," she says. Her eyes dart about my face. "What are you worried about?"

"I killed MacGee." This time I do see her flinch.

"Your friend," she says or asks. "You mean you got him caught?"

"No. They were torturing him," I say, pause. It's hard to sift through such memories and pull them out so that they can be turned into words. Whatever chemical makeup these memories have, it's reacting with my body, eating it, and my muscles shiver in response. I stare at her face. Some micro hairs, sprout from her cheek. This only makes me want her more. But this visual opiate is easily defeated as I think again about what's just happened in the past few hours. I'm reminded of a parasite that slowly takes over crabs. The crab, upon contact, trembles violently trying to get rid of the invader. To no avail. The crab will live, and in fact not deteriorate in health until the parasite has fully taken control of the entire body. I tremble again as I think of MacGee. My friend. The moment we talked alone in his dark room.

Genevine's eyes urge me to go on. Perhaps saying it will help. My body shivers again. "I walked in. Talked to him and shot him."

Though she doesn't move, I see her distancing herself from me. That was the wrong thing to say. Is this connection that I just thought would last a lifetime, already over?

"Why?" she asks. "Your friend."

"I didn't…" I think about if I should tell her all my intentions. She's slipping away, and I'm at that point where I could pull back as well, or try to win her back with the truth. Something from my heart.

"I couldn't stand to see him get tortured again. They were going to take him apart, one piece at a time. I couldn't…"

She has a tender look on her face. "I'm sorry," she says.

"Have they always tortured people like this?"

"That's always been the case with an enemy, right?"

I don't agree, but history seems to point that way. "True," I say. MacGee didn't agree with that.

She moves in and muzzles my neck. It's as if her doing something's what makes me like it. There's no spark. Have I spent all my love on Carol, and Jenny? I think of telling Genevine about Jenny, maybe just Carol. I don't. What is it that I'm trying to accomplish? I hold Genevine closer to me and smell her skin. Sweat, with the hint of soap. I'm home and slowly dreams take over.

"Hi," Genevine says, leaning over me. "Do you want some breakfast?"

I yawn and stretch out. I want something more and pull her in. I have an inkling that my last dream was about me running. From whom? I kiss her, feel down on her thighs. Thick, supple. I want to be nice. I should, but she's here and I don't sense any rejection in her.

"The others are here," she whispers into my ear.

I glance at the door, it's closed. I hear the burst of laughter in the distance. That doesn't deter me. But if she doesn't want to… I know what happened with Jenny and I won't do that again.

"No?" I ask.

She smiles, and rolls her eyes.

The warmth she wraps me in grabs my chest, my balls and it's over as I crumple over. She smiles when I'm done. I'm breathing hard, and she hops up. "I'll get breakfast ready for you?"

"All right," I say.

I get my clothes ready then lie back down on the bed. I don't want to go out there. I have no idea what to expect. Will there be a mob outside my house? John leading them to take me to the torture chamber? And if not, what else can I do? I've just killed the only friend I've ever had. I close my eyes. I see Jenny on the edge of the cliff. I see MacGee, his eyes closed and the slide of the handgun as I pulled the trigger. Then the moment we sat and talked. That connection. My wife Carol, the last sunset we spent together. The memories start running together. Not the visual aspects, but the emotion, the way the heart beat to each moment.

I'm back there and I don't want to live in the now. What's gotten in me? Am I scared of John? Why? I've gone through so much to get here, and yet... I'm scared of changing again. My eyes well up, and I fight back the tears. Do I want to end up like Jenny? MacGee? They'd been too soft. I remember what begging in front of a gun did. Nothing. Not once. I've made it this far. But this is different; I can't very well try to waste every man who I think's against me.

And who is against me? I have to find that out. And I have to find a few friends. The numbers game. And yet, haven't I found a home? What's wrong with finding a place here and growing old with Genevine by my side? My memories seem to be the kind that will fight this, but memories fade, don't they?

I walk into the kitchen and see Genevine and three other women, the same ones from before, or so I think, around the table.

"You ready?" Genevine says, with a little too much confidence.

I grunt and sit in front of some oatmeal. It tastes like it's been cooked with dirt, but I don't complain. They've all finished so they look at me like they want me to say something. I look up between bites and slowly develop an avuncular feel for them.

"Thanks," I say when I'm finished. I pause. I can feel my handgun pushing into my waist. I'll keep that, but I need more bullets. I walk out without saying anything to them.

"Where are the scouts headed to?" I ask. I'm at the gate and there are two trucks being mounted up with men.

25

"They've found another group of enemies," the gate guard says. He seems to be happy, as well as mentally stunted.

"Oh?" I say and look for John. "Where's John?"

The guard shrugs his head. "You going with them?"

I look at the camp. I don't want to be here, do I? No, I'd rather be with these men.

Why though? They tried to rape that woman, didn't they? The other Tom. Thomas. They made me a liar. No, these are the kind of thoughts that will eat away at you. This is the group you've chosen, they have God on their side, and they're doing the best they can. How can you be angry with them for killing others when you've killed too?

The gate opens. I move in front of the first truck. "I want to come with," I say to the driver.

He looks at me like I'm a fool.

"This is only recon," he says, as if that means anything to me.

I shrug, try to act as hard as possible. "I don't care. I want to come."

He shrugs back. "You can do what you want. It's a free country." He grins, flashes yellow and black teeth. Something about him agrees with me.

I shake his hand. "Tom."

"I know," he says. He has blue eyes like the rest, and dirty blonde hair. He seems to be gentle of heart.

"You?"

"Brad," he says. I'm just here to drive." He smiles like he can't help it.

And I can't help but smile back.

"Tom."

I turn. It's John, beaming, as if he's proud that I'm here. "Hi," I say. We embrace, and it's for a few seconds. I smell some sort of sweet spice on him. I think back to what he said in that abode alone with me. He does care. And how can I blame him for going against MacGee? MacGee had tried to kill him. What have I done to people who tried the same with me? Bill; Jenny's family; the other family near the remains of Portland. I feel guilt, but replace it with understanding for John's actions.

And almost by magic the memories that have been eating me up dissolve.

"You're coming with us?" John asks.

"I will," I say. "We're expanding the Kingdom, aren't we?"

"Yes, you'll ride with me."

We jump in the back of the first truck's cab and John taps Brad's shoulder. "You know where, right?"

Soon I'm looking at the desert landscape passing us by. It's beautiful in a stark way. If I pretend not to know that this is the place that provides no food, I can love it. There's nothing but a cloud of dust behind us. I lean over to John. "Won't someone see us from a mile away?"

John pats my back. "Don't worry, this will be fine."

I keep quiet and look behind us at the truck bed. There are at least twenty men holding on for dear life. They too stare at the passing land. Though some are just trying to protect their faces from the driving dust. I cough when some sand enters my lungs.

"Who are we going after?" I ask. I remember the map John showed me.

"An enemy," John says with a smile.

How do you know, is something I want to ask, but I decide not to. "Good."

When I move my feet, I kick an assault rifle. I pick it up.

"You want one?" John asks.

"Of course," I say.

"It's yours," he says. There's something in his voice, the excitement perhaps, that reminds me of a child on the way to a great vacation.

"Thanks." My chest swells up, and I return to staring at the landscape. We drive for an hour through landscape that I've never seen before. Then we take a left into some cracked mountains. Soon we're on an incline. The truck rolls from side to side, and at one point I'm looking directly down a cliff. The boys in the back don't seem to mind it, so I hold on and stare at the horizon. It steadies me.

As we climb higher, I can see more of the land, the distant untouchable horizon. Hazy peaks shimmer, and the border, where sky and land meet, waivers like mercury. Close up the rocks are jagged and cracked, almost like worlds of their own. Again the horizon jumps forward and the curvature of the planet bends to include me. I'm not sure why, but I'm overwhelmed, and as my heart increases in size, I hold back involuntary tears. I remember the Lord's Prayer when I was a child, and I remember saying it with Samantha's family only a short while ago.

I can't believe the hate and contempt I held. I can't believe that MacGee was going to make me hate all this. He was a friend, but he also didn't believe in the same things as I did. He didn't believe in God and that made him weak. It'd made Jenny weak. And that's the way of the world.

"You all right?" John asks and taps me.

I turn to him, the truck lurches to his side and forces me to come within a few inches of his face. "I'm fine," I say.

He places his hand on my shoulder. For a brief moment what swirls in the space between us are all the lies I told him last night, all the times I confronted him because I hated him, and I wonder why I'm not angry with him this very moment.

"Tom, remember that God takes care of his flock. All right?" He smiles.

I nod. And all that dirt swirling between us melts away. Gone forever. I smile back, feel a chord form between us. John has been my friend. He's helped me and believes in the Lord same as I do. "I know," I say. The warm feeling, the touch of God that I felt before expands. I pull John towards me and hug him. I can feel him stiffen then relax.

"We are brothers for life, aren't we?" I say.

We separate, John looking at me like he's not sure what to expect of me.

"Of course," he says. "Always."

I smile, and feeling like I'm on the brink of breaking up, turn to my window. Now there's a drop off that I stare at. Vertigo engulfs me. The call of the fall, like before. *She* took it. But I could never, no matter how long and softly it called my name. And the memory of Jenny comes up, not her beautiful body, or her eyes, or the warmth as I thrust in, but her deriding stare, how it made me feel. And this emotion, this collection of chemicals whispers in my ear: "you fool" and I push it away by staring at the horizon.

Anger grows from this collision of ideas.

Something's working up in my stomach, but my mind takes over and I swear to myself that I'll do something grand. Not like last time where I was credited with something I didn't deserve. I'll do so much better this time. I'll help build something, and if that takes some violence, then so be it. I knew how to do it before, and I'll be able to do it again.

The truck finally hits a plateau and we slow to a creep. John leans over.

"We're getting close," he says.

I fix my eyes ahead, hold the rifle in my hand, then remember that I've never fired this kind before. I look at John and he grins and shows me the slide and how to release the safety and magazine.

"Very easy," he says. I like him even more. Finally, we come to a halt.

"Send the scouts ahead," John says. I watch as three men gather up some of their things and feel a pang of jealousy.

"I'll go with them," I say.

John looks me up and down. He seems to understand, more than me, because I'm not certain where this desire comes from.

"Of course," he says.

I get out and follow the men. They look like men I haven't met before, though they could be the same men in that cave with Thomas. They give me grunts of approval, as if they didn't expect this, and they let me fall in behind them. None of them talk.

We come to the tip of a ridge, and they start slouching. I do the same. My insides simmer. I tense up considering what's next. Did I really sign up for more of this violence? I don't consider that thought for long as the three scouts crawl to their bellies, and I do the same. We're looking over a cliff edge. Below us unfurls a valley. This one is also protected on all sides by fingers of rocks rising several hundred feet up into the sky.

One of the scouts, a skinny young man with a carved face, pulls out his binoculars and adjusts them. The rest look hard in the same direction. I follow their line of sight and see nothing.

The other two men without binoculars are on either side of me. I tap one and curl my fingers to ask what it is we're looking at. The man, slightly chubby and no taller than me, doesn't seem the least bit perturbed.

"The group lives down there among the rocks. We watched them a few days back and saw that they only come out when necessary. I think they still think the air isn't safe."

There's derision in that last sentence, and I absorb it. "How many?"

"No idea. At least ten."

I look at the black mouths of what must be caves. If they are living down there they must not have much more to eat. "How many entrances?" I ask. I'm trying to formulate a plan, but don't know how to go about it. I have it in my mind that I'll impress these men with my ability.

"Three, last time we counted."

I take deep gulps to calm down my heart. I wonder if the people have any inkling that they're being watched. Then I think about how we were watched before. John never said what they saw. Had I been seen with Samantha? I try to focus on the mission at hand.

"There," the skinny scout with the binoculars says.

I squint and can see some movement. Out crawls a figure from one of the holes. It comes out like it knows there can't be anything alive in the world and walks with a limp. Behind it another two figures come out behind it. I take them to be men, only because of their size and more certain gait. The first figure, which now looks like a woman, turns back to the other two and beckons them to come her. She points out something on the ground.

"Dammit," the skinny scout says.

"What is it?"

"You dropped a wrapper when we crept up there at night," the skinny one says to the chubby one next to me.

"It wasn't me," the chubby one says, his voice narrowing to a squeak.

On my other side is an older, also skinny man, and he growls in a low, rusted voice: "Shut up you two."

His face has the markings of sandpaper and old fights. He clenches his jaw, and his whole head flashes lines of solemnity.

"Mitt," the old man says. "You really left a wrapper there?"

Mitt, the chubby one, shakes his head vigorously. "I—"

The old man raises his hand and turns to the skinny one, on his other side. "What kind of wrapper, Craig?"

"Snickers," Craig says, still staring through his binos.

"Jim," Mitt says, his voice almost loud. "I—"

"Shut up, you worthless fat fuck," Jim, the old man, growls and reaches over me to slap Mitt on his head. His forearm hits me in the process. "Sorry, Tom." His voice is tinged with deference. I imagine it's because he knows I'm John's friend.

"Not to worry," I whisper.

"What are they doing?" Jim asks.

"Picking it up and looking around."

"Stay still, everyone."

I hold my breath as the three figures below twist their necks trying to find someone. At this point I wonder why the woman had walked out so confidently. She must have suspected the possibility of someone else around.

"When they leave we'll slowly back off," Jim says under his breath.

But they don't leave. Instead three more people crawl out of a hole and join them. They spread out and start looking. It reminds me of animals scavenging. We're at least a couple hundred feet above them. They could start climbing the rocks.

Without warning, they group back together and climb back down their hole.

"Now," Jim says. One by one we crawl back as slowly as possible. When we're out of sight we sit up.

"You went down there?" I ask Mitt.

31

"We all did," Jim said. "I wanted to see if we could sneak down those holes."

Another glance at him, and I can see that he's tough, a man made for fighting. Craig seems the same, though he seems to lack the badge of experience. Mitt doesn't look like he fits at all. Perhaps he joined the scouts because they get extra rations.

"Did you?"

"I managed to look down one. The one they all walked out of."

I picture him lowering himself in to the hole. I can't imagine how.

"And?" I ask.

"There was a guard," Jim says. "Luckily he was asleep."

"So they expect people to jump them?" I say.

"That's right. We saw them with a slave. A captured man."

I pause. "You think they fought another group?"

"We know. There was one close by that we knew about. A day ago we went there and there was nothing," Jim says.

"Stripped clean," Mitt adds, his voice sad.

"Some blood on the rocks," Craig adds.

"How many?" I ask.

"At least ten," Jim says.

"And they were probably killed," I say.

Jim looks at me like I'm silly. "Used. For food, or energy. The one we saw was tied up, and they were pretty brutal with him."

"Ate him?" I ask. My throat shivers, my head shrinks.

Jim nods. Mitt and Craig slouch away.

"That's why John wants to take them out," I add in a whisper.

Jim eyes narrow at me. He shakes his head. I move to ask him what that means, but he's up and away. I follow him.

Back with John, we huddle around a piece of paper that Jim pulls out. It's a makeshift map of the place we just saw.

"So no count?" John asks.

"They might know we're in the area," Jim adds, in a way that doesn't have the same deferent tone he used with me.

I can see John's forearms clench.

"How's that?" John's voice cuts the air hard. It shakes me out of a thought that perhaps Carol is being used as a slave right now.

Jim shrugs. "They're good." He glances at me. "Aren't they?"

"Of course," I say.

John takes this well. "All right. But do they know how many we are, any of that?"

"No," Jim says and raises his hand. "They just know there's someone out there. Maybe one person who they need to be on the lookout for."

"We should hit them fast and hard," I add.

"We should..." John says and looks at me with the same face as when we embraced.

"Very well," John says.

Jim nods his head, pats me on my back. "This is what I'm talking about. Let's hit them now."

John raises his hand. "We don't have much by way of flame thrower fuel."

Jim spits on the ground. His posture towards John borders on insolent, but no one says anything.

"We can get them, the same way you get a damn rattlesnake out of its hole," says Jim.

"Tom, what do you think?" John asks.

I sense hostility.

"I think we should cover all the exits." I think on what I would hate to see if I'm one of those holes. "Use the flame throwers on as many as possible. It's my guess that they're all attached. When they come running out we..." I pause and look around. Everyone seems to be taking me seriously. "Shoot them."

A grumble of approval goes up. Jim pats me again. "Atta boy, that's what I'm talking about."

The other two scouts also pat me on the back. My chest swells. I feel invincible.

"Very good, Tom," John says. "Then I'll watch from up top and you take care of this."

I wonder if this is a challenge.

"Sounds good." I turn to Jim. "How many flamethrowers do we have?"

"Five," John says in the background.

"Get them and have them in front of whichever exits were used most. And at least one person on the other exits."

Jim nods. I look at him for a second, hoping that he will carry most of the work for me. If it's details that are needed, I'm lost.

Jim spins and starts barking orders. I see Mitt and Craig punch through the group of ragtag soldiers and mutter orders to them. Soon Jim's in front of a map and pointing out where everyone'll go.

We all head out. John and a couple other men stay with the trucks. I think they're from the council, but I don't ask. My head's bursting with thoughts of what could go wrong. Are the people whom we saw down there ready for this? They'd seen the wrapper and they'd, without warning, disappeared.

I lead the group with Jim next to me. I can feel my feet and head floating.

"Don't worry, Tom," Jim says when we're out of earshot. "This will be a piece of cake."

"I have no doubts," I say, then wonder if I'm being too cocky. After all, though I'm in charge, this is Jim's show.

We walk down a narrow cut draw. It's deep enough that it covers most of our movements. When we get close to the bowl—where the cave entrances are—the draw shallows out and we slouch, then crawl on our bellies. Jim turns to the other men, and speaks in a loud whisper: "All right men, on my word we'll rush to our positions. Craig, Mitt, point out their holes."

I nod furiously, like this is all according to my plan. There's a double squeeze on my brain from the danger that I could be facing, as well as the men around me looking down upon me. I've done this before, I remind myself, I've put men into the dirt to be here, and I can keep on doing it. That thought pumps my balls for a boost of energy.

With one swift motion I leap up and follow Jim who's already a few feet ahead of me. I'll stay next to him for the duration of this fight.

I expect the people who live in these holes to come out and meet our charge, but they don't. I stop behind Jim when he takes a knee several feet before the main entrance. He grins at me when I place a hand on his shoulder.

"You're a calm one, aren't you?" he asks.

I'm nervous as hell, but decide to smile. "Let's do this," I say as I taste blood. A young man pulls up next to me with a flamethrower. I see fear in his eyes. He's trying to stay between us and the holes.

"Get up here," Jim growls and yanks the man over.

I see Craig and Mitt's eyes trained on Jim. A quiet echoes across my world. Jim raises his hand and orange flames lick out and disappear down the holes. I have a quick feeling of excitement. We're doing this; we're going to defeat these bastards. And as the air around the holes cackles, my elation drops. My heart drops, and I feel numb. I remember Thomas and his men. I remember the trust he had in me. The look on his face. The look on MacGee's face. But MacGee was a fool, I try to tell myself. It doesn't work.

Jim snaps his finger in front of my face.

"Train your gun on those two holes. You see someone come out, shoot them."

I move my gun. MacGee was a fool who didn't know how to survive. Pure and simple. Jenny too. God's Kingdom, and we all had to play by His rules.

The screams start.

"Move forward," Jim says, and the flamethrowers step up to the holes. The screams grow louder. I can hear the higher pitches of a girl, maybe a woman. Then a man. The boy with the flamethrower giggles. He looks nervous. There are two holes that I'm staring at. I pray that no one comes out. I spit on the ground.

The screaming now reverberates in my chest. I hear a bang. I turn and see a flame-licked man fly out of the hole in front of Jim and collapse at our feet.

Jim kicks the flickering corpse. The man's meat smells fresh, grilled, sweet. My stomach rumbles. I feel sick. I try to focus on my two holes. Don't let anyone get by. Smoke's billowing out of one of the holes.

A head peeks out from the non-smoking one. I cock my head and raise my rifle. The head disappears. A silence settles. Then screaming starts again. It's from the hole with smoke coming out of it. A hand pops out of it. I stare. It slowly turns into the crawling, blackened torso of a man, with cracks of red. An odd chortling sound comes out of him. Charred, every movement looks like a moment of insurmountable pain. I feel my knees buckling. I can't. Not here with everyone around.

I fire a shot. Dust kicks up around the man. He doesn't react. A gurgling sound comes forth from his mouth. I start firing, because the sound and the man's position on the ground, all worm into my brain. A few shots later, and the man falls over. I fire again. He stops moving.

What are we doing here? I stare at the blackened human flesh.

"All right," Jim says, and I feel the heat from the flamethrower dissipating.

I see the head pop out of the hole again. It appears to be the head of a girl, but disappears before I can be certain.

Jim has two men walk into the holes that have just been torched. I'm taking deep breaths, trying not to think about the crawling motion of the man I just shot. A few minutes later, I hear the men come out of the caves affirming that everyone's dead.

"Let's move out," Jim says, with a large grin on his face. "I'll get a count of dead bodies in a second."

The man with the flamethrower looks at the charred body of the man I shot.

"I'm surprised he made it that far," he says and whistles.

I try to grin, but my face revolts.

"Good shot," the flamethrower man says and elbows me. "The ones in there are charred beyond belief. I mean just melted." He chuckles again.

I'm thinking that he's not right in the head. That he couldn't possibly be enjoying this. Then I see a crack in his smile. For the briefest of seconds the man's face seems to flash a shriek of pain, before returning to his foolish grin.

"All of them?" I ask.

"All of them." He chuckles again, then looks off.

The smell of grilled meat is in the air, and I walk to the charred man I shot. He's facing the sky and only his eyes aren't burned. Or not burned beyond recognition. His eyelids are burned off, and his mouth is agape. Tears rush up, and I push them back down. Jenny's face is coming to me. Jenny's innocence too. This is what I am, isn't it?

Jim comes up to me. "Seemed like a fighter," he says.

"There's one more hole," I say.

"No," the flamethrower man says. "The other hole leads out here, I saw this burned bastard's feet from inside. There's nothing more."

"There is at least one more person," I reply and point to the hole where I saw the head pop out and in.

"Damn," Jim says. "Alive?"

"That's right," I say. And even though I'm sick to my stomach of charred flesh. Can't really believe I've taken part in this travesty, my mind speaks up for me. "Stick a flamethrower in there. That should get them out."

"We're out of fuel," the flamethrower man says.

I glare at him.

"We'll have to go in," Jim says and pulls out a handgun. The man with the flamethrower steps back. The other men are around us now and looking confused. A murmur rises.

"I need one more," Jim says. Everyone's eyes cast down and they step back.

I feel a few stares. "I'll go," I say. I shoulder my rifle. Jim sneers at me while smiling at the same time. It's an odd look. He hands me a flashlight. Pushing past Jim, I step to the hole and head in. With the light on, I crouch and duck-walk into a large tunnel. I can hear water dripping. I can smell sweat and feces. Every inch that the light reveals, I expect to see a barrel sparking back at me.

"Easy," Jim whispers behind me. His hand on my shoulder, he gently tugs me back. But I don't want to let him steal the glory. I don't know why, but the fear in my bones is morphing into something that makes me want to charge forward. Not care. Am I hoping for a punishment?

One step and I hear the distinct sound of hushed words. Jim grabs my flashlight and, pushing it down, turns it off.

"Don't make a sound."

I feel my blood expanding my arteries. I don't care. I move on. One foot in front of the other. Behind me Jim's breathing is labored. He sounds like an old man. I hope he doesn't shoot me if this becomes a gunfight. I remember those four men I put into the dirt with Jenny. I won then; I'll win this too.

The voices, hushed, echo off the wall, and now I'm sure that there're people only a few feet away. I take another step and the air cools. The sounds are less constrictive. This must be the main cave, but I can't see anything. The don't care attitude I just had is gone. I'm scared again. Is there someone else just a few feet away?

I try to make out any shape. A whisper breaks out and echoes off a wall. I can't tell where it's coming from. Nothing but blackness around me, and I turn my head back and forth. I'm not moving now since I assume that I'll step on someone, or something. I can hear Jim behind me breathing. Surely they can hear that?

A spark blinds the left half of my vision. The sound is like a bark, a violent scream. I flinch, and my ears burst into a whine. I fall to the ground, pulling the trigger on my rifle and seeing shapes form in front of me as I fire. Two men with guns. I fire at them. I see their eyes wide.

They fly back, and another gun starts up. It lights up the other half of this cave. I see Jim firing it. I follow what he's shooting, but there's nothing but crates. I half smile, knowing that he's as scared as me. But he keeps spraying the crates.

"Stop!" I yell. I half expect him to shoot me, but I move to his side and yell in his ear. "Stop!"

Silence erupts. I fumble for my flashlight. I remember stuffing it into a pocket when Jim turned it off, but I can't find it.

A light comes on. It's Jim with a flare. The room is clear now. One dark hole is the only exit, the place we came through, and crates are splintered everywhere. Blood's splattered on the wall as well as white gooey pieces of matter—I don't want to know.

"Good shot," Jim says as he walks over to the bodies. I make it over to him and stare at the faces, eyes still open, staring through us. I feel sorry for them. I look back up the dark hole we came from. Something in me is glad we risked our lives to shoot them. Not glad to take their lives, but to offer something other than seeing a flame screeching and burning them alive. I shiver.

A crate moves. Jim spins to it, with his handgun, and I grab his arm. No more death, I think, but have enough sense not to say it. A small cry comes up. I walk over and see a little girl, her hands covering her face. Small sobs leak out of her face. She can't be more than ten years old. I reach out to her and with surprising quickness a knife slashes out at me. I move my hand in time and only get scratched. I'm faster than her, so I reach back in and grab her wrist. She tries to squirm, but I pick her up and shake the knife out of her hand. It falls to the floor and the girl stops kicking. She stares at me. There isn't an ounce of fear in her.

"Oh, it's a feisty one, is it?" Jim says. He raises his handgun. "Let me finish her off."

"Don't," I say and raise my hand. Jim gives me a look.

"Why not? She just tried to kill you."

"She's scared," I say.

"Of course she is. She's about to die."

The girl starts to kick and scream. She bites into my hand. I slap her, silencing her. I grab her hair and push her to the ground. "Stay still, will you?" Her eyes are full of hate.

"Tom, I know it's tough. But you've got to finish her. We just…" He jerks his head to the two bodies. "Her entire clan. She's not going to take that lightly, is she?"

I'm not so sure. Didn't I read somewhere that the ancients used to take in the children of the clans they took over?

I stare at the girl. She does have the look that she wants to end me, the moment she gets the chance. "Are you going to kill me?" I ask her.

A gobble of spit comes flying out of her mouth and lands on my cheek. I wipe it off, as Jim steps forward, his fist raised.

"You little brat, I'll show you."

"Jim!" I say and Jim stops in his tracks. "Let me deal with this. Search the rest of the room and tell me what you find."

"Look at your folks," Jim says to the girl, ignoring me. "You'll soon be like them."

"Jim!" I yell, resisting the urge to grab him by his throat. "Did you hear me?"

Jim shrugs and starts shuffling around the room, kicking boxes around.

"You have a choice. Behave, or die," I say to the girl. "Do you understand?"

The girl blinks. I see her hard face crack into softness.

"Do you understand? Because it's either me, or him. And he'll end your life very easily."

I hear Jim come to a stop.

"You find something Jim?"

"No," he says and goes back to kicking things.

I've some apprehension about pissing Jim off, but since I did all the dirty work in this tunnel I know I have some leeway. I stare at the girl. "You have to decide now."

"Are they dead?" she asks, her voice is that of a scared child's. Jim stops moving, and I hear his flare move closer.

"Everyone else is dead," I say.

It's hard to gauge her reaction. She doesn't seem shocked, but the wheels in her mind are turning. Is she thinking about revenge? That's a possibility, in fact I can't see her feeling anything else, and yet I don't care. I want her to be okay. I want her to take my hand. And even if it means a knife in my back, I'll take that risk just to be her caregiver.

"Were your parents one of them?" I ask.

She shakes her head. "My family."

I reach for her hand. She pulls away, her eyes glaring. I smell blood, the sharp chemical of the flares, and feces from the corpses. Though this plants me firmly in the now, I can't help but see Jenny in the girl's eyes, her hate for me. This softens me and I raise my hands, palms out. "You have my word I won't hurt you. But understand what happens when you choose not come with us. All right?" I'm perfectly aware that as a child she might not have the slightest clue as to the consequences of her action. Perhaps she doesn't know revenge either. She is a girl, isn't she? My mind shoots to an encyclopedia about the ancients who would cut all the testes of the young men they captured. That way those men wouldn't be a problem.

"I'm with you," she says.

"Tom," Jim says, his voice seems to have softened. "You can take her with us, but don't let her out of your sight."

"Why?" I ask, though I half know the answer.

"Make sure they know she's yours. Otherwise they'll take her away," he says and leans in to whisper. "Even your friend John. Some of these sickos like 'em young."

I can't imagine John like that. Actually I'm sure that none of them are like that. "All right," I say.

Raising my hands to shield off the daylight, I walk out to some applause.

"What did you two find?"

"You can scrounge for some food," Jim says and points to two other men who head down the entrance.

"Oh lookie here," another man says and grabs the girl.

I haven't kept her close because I assumed that she would be all right. Luckily she's wearing a pink dress, and I find and reach out for her. Three men are pawing at her, while some others look on and laugh. She struggles.

"Stop," I say and place my hand on one of the men who has his hand up her skirt.

He gives me a look that gives me pause. He's a rough looking man, long tattered brown hair, wide jawed and with breath that smells like rotted meat. I remember my strength.

"You heard me. She's mine," I say.

"All finds from the enemy are for the taking," he says, showing me his yellow and brown teeth. His eyes glare at me, and his hand moves further up the girl's skirt. She lets out a stifled scream and wiggles. Anger starts to bubble up.

I reach for my rifle, then decide that wouldn't be prudent. I squeeze the man's shoulder. "I found her. She's mine. Next time you walk down a fucking tunnel, I'll let you keep whatever you find."

The man steps back, his hands still on the girl.

"Let him have her," Jim growls from behind me. For a second, I'm not sure if he's talking to me or the man.

"You heard me," Jim says and steps up beside me. "Tom here mowed down two men not but a few feet away from him. In the dark." I can hear a round of approval go up with the men surrounding us. The other two men with hands on the girl step back.

The man with the hand up her skirt doesn't budge. He narrows his eyes at me. I feel my balls pumping my muscles with energy. I'll have to take him down. I move one foot forward. Then I wonder how I'll do it without hurting the girl. I back off.

"Let her go," Jim says, his finger pointing at the man. "Or everyone here will know about the time you were in a firefight and how you pissed your pants."

The man shrinks back, and I see his hand move away from the girl. A few snickers rise up out of the others.

"I said," Jim shouts, his voice echoes off the cliff.

The man steps back, pushes the girl to the ground and walks off.

I walk over to the girl. All the men still have predatory eyes zeroing in on her. I can't be too nice to her. I grab her hand and hold tight.

"That was impressive," John says. He's only a few feet away. He must have come down when he was sure that nothing violent was going to happen. He claps.

"Thank you," I say.

John smiles at me. "You shot two of them when they were a few feet away?"

Jim steps up. "It was the craziest thing I've ever seen. We were at the bottom of the cave," Jim says and places a hand on my back. "And Tom here was in front of me. I could hear them breathing." The other men move in to hear this. Even I lean in, because Jim is barely whispering, and I want to hear about what just happened.

"Right next to my face." He raises his hand to his face to indicate the distance. "And I'm thinking that this is the end of ol' Jim. That I can't see my enemy, and I haven't got a prayer against whoever has been living in this hole for years."

It's as if everyone's holding their breath.

"I was so nervous that my hands were sweating. I wasn't even certain that I could hold my gun anymore. It almost slipped right there. Luckily it didn't drop because then the others would have gotten a bead on me in a heart beat." Jim shakes his head slowly. "And I was thinking, what the hell did I get myself into this? I couldn't even see where ol' Tom was. If I was to shoot, I'd hit him. I actually thought that we should back up, get the hell out of there," Jim says looking at everyone, incredulous at his own actions. "I was scared out of my wits, and was about to feel with my hands for Tom and retreat."

A short murmur goes up amongst the group. Everyone's looking at Jim with approval. Me too. The girl's grip tightens. And it was then that the fear, that the few doubts—which might be the same thing as the fear—swimming in my blood, starts to morph into something else. I feel a pull to the men, John, Jim. And I feel like I… I'm not sure, but I feel the best I've felt since I dug myself out of the cave.

"There I am trying to think about the ways I have to stop from pissin' my pants, when the first guns lit up." Jim shakes the crowd by yelling the last part and whipping his hands out. "Down there when someone shoots, it's loud. And again. I could see the faces of these buggers. Only a few feet away. Them just as fast as me. And what do I do? I freeze. I reach for my handgun and my hands are sweating so much that I can't grip my gun properly." Jim spits, shaking his head, and grabs my hand. "And who saved the fucking day?" He raises my hand. "I couldn't see Tom here. But he had dived out of the way. And only a split second after these bastards had started to fire, did he fire back."

I'm staring at the ground because looking up might make me blush. I feel the girl squeezing tight on my hand, and I wonder how she feels, knowing that this is a story about the end of her people. I steel myself and look up. There are a few eyes on me, and they immediately move off me. Heads nod at me with scrunched up chins of approval. I forget about the girl and feel powerful. I'm the star for now, and it feels good. The thoughts about the charred bodies melt away.

"And man within a second he laid down some fire and those boys who were trying to end us, didn't speak no more." Jim says, his tone, voice changing into something surprisingly contemplative. "Tom here is a goddamn hero. When he finished, both were dead. Never stood a chance."

John steps forward. "Thank you Jim." He places an arm on my other shoulder. "It's safe to say that Tom here has proven himself again."

A chorus of yeses goes up.

"And," John continues, "Has shown the rest of us how we need to fight for the Kingdom of God!"

A roar sounds, and I feel a rain of slaps on my body.

"And is this your booty?" John asks and leans over to the girl. Some of the men laugh.

There's something about the look on John's face that rubs against my bones. The girl squeezes my hand, and her other hand grabs my thigh. Yet, from the look in everyone's eyes, I know that I still can't be nice to her.

"Looks like she wants you bad," John says and lets out a laugh. "Is that right little girl?"

I want to intervene, but don't. I smile, and force out a chuckle. John's look has a hunger to it. I can't let this girl leave my sight.

"What about it?" John asks again, and his face hardens, stares at the girl like he wants her to say something wrong. There's no way I can let him keep poking her. And yet I can't show any softness to her.

"Don't worry John," I say. "I'll teach her a few lessons in manners. She's my dog."

John straightens himself out and smiles with half his mouth. He's thinking. What, though? "I have no doubt that you will, Tom."

We head back to the trucks. I can see more of the sky, in fact some of it's bluer than anything I've ever seen before; things will get better. The girl clings on to me the entire ride back. I jump in on a truck that isn't John's. I hung back to make sure that his was seated and for others to get in with him before I moved to an open seat. I can handle the other guys because I can kick them off the girl. But if John starts to fondle her, like I'm sure he will, I can't push his hand away.

The sun sets, lighting up the sky with a red and orange that replaces the air in my lungs with awe and contemplation. I provide a quiet receptacle for all the compliments of the men around me. I catch the girl staring at me a few times. I almost sense some affection. What a horrid choice I've given her: die or hang on to the man who murdered those who love you. I'm thinking of the Bible story about the good Samaritan and I can't seem to apply it to my situation. That story was about a good man. I'm not.

I walk into my house, with the night settling on the village, threatening wretched dreams. I take one look behind me to make sure that no one is there to see me, or possibly follow me to ask questions. When the trucks came in everyone was there to meet them. I saw some of the women cast the girl a few angry eyes. I realize that I haven't asked John what the ratio of women to men is here.

As the door slams behind me, and I make sure to lock the bolt, the girl tries to break my grip on her arm. I hold on. There are still women in here, or there could be, and they won't take kindly to an outsider if the looks on the other women's faces were any indication.

"Hold on," I say and drag her into the kitchen. I feel her heel hit me right behind my knee. One leg goes out from under me. I barely manage to stay up. Furious, I pull her face close to mine. "Listen here, you little…" I take a deep breath when I see fear on her face. "You need to act right, or else I'll kick you out to them." I stop when I see her face cracking into a cry. I'm supposed to at least try to be good, right? "Do you understand? I'm sorry about what happened, but you have to deal with it, all right?"

"I want life the way it was before," the girl says.

Those words cut into me.

"Deal with what?"

I turn to Genevine.

"Are the others here?"

"It's just us," Genevine replies, and cocks her head.

"Where did they go?" I ask, looking around.

"There's a meeting at the main hall in a little bit," she smiles at me. "I think it's about you."

I remain still. For some reason all the backslapping from the other men feels… facile in front of Genevine.

"Ohhh, have you been out playing war with the boys again?" she says in a cooing voice.

Before I can answer the girl struggles trying to break my grip.

"What's this?" Genevine asks and moves closer to me.

"She was with the group we conquered," I say. Though massacred would have been a better word.

Genevine's eyes parse the girl. It's hard to tell what exactly her motivation is. Does she like the girl? Is she like everyone else? No, she can't be.

"She's mine," I say and the girl takes this as an opportunity to kick me in the shins. I let her go, and she breaks as if to run, then stops and turns a few feet from both of us.

"Oh no she isn't," Genevine says.

I can't tell what she means.

I look at the girl who's regarding us both with a meanness that speaks of her future revenge.

"Isn't that right?" Genevine asks the girl. "You're nobody's, right?"

The girl doesn't answer, though her eyes soften at Genevine.

"What do you mean?" I ask.

"I mean, she's a person, and no one, not least you, owns her," Genevine snaps at me.

"Well," I say feeling slighted at Genevine's words. "If I don't take her in, the others will tear her apart."

"Of course they will. They're idiots. And," she says and turns to the girl. "You are more than welcome to stay with us. But you are your own person, aren't you?"

The girl takes a second to look at me with distaste and nods her head at Genevine.

"Fine," I say. My emotions catch up to the realization that this means Genevine is fine with having the girl, though I'm still stinging from her words.

"Are you hungry?" Genevine asks.

"Yeah," I reply.

"Not you, the girl. What's your name?" she asks. When the girl doesn't answer, Genevine looks at me. I shrug.

"You didn't find out?" Genevine says.

I follow, my stomach now rumbling. Genevine pulls out some stew from a pot on the stove. "They say the farming isn't going as well as they thought. That there will be less rations soon."

I watch as she only takes one plate out. Angry with Genevine for still pulling this game with me, I walk to the cupboard and grab a bowl for myself.

The girl sniffs the food before she starts to swallow it. Genevine smiles. "Eat slowly. Chew. No one's going to take this away from you."

"We should keep her here for the ceremony," I say.

Genevine nods. "I'll stay here with her. You go. To. Your ceremony."

Something has come over her. I decide to let it be. Perhaps she saw me treating the girl too roughly. That was fine. As long as she was willing to help me take care of her.

"Rusty," the girl says. Her voice shakes us both out of our silences.

"What?" I ask.

"Rusty."

"The food?" I say and take another taste. This time I'm sure that I can taste rust. I give Genevine a raised eyebrow.

"Rusty," the girl says and points her spoon at her chest.

"Your name is Rusty," Genevine says and kicks me from under the table.

"That's no name," I say. I receive another kick from Genevine.

"It's a perfectly acceptable name. Your parents name you that?"

The girl nods.

"I'm Genevine."

The girl nods.

"I'm Tom." I scarf down the rest of my food.

"I know," the girl says.

Genevine smiles.

"I like her."

I shrug. "I'll be back," I say and head out to the main hall.

A the ceremony, John sings my praises to all high hell. But when the whole crowd roars and surges forth as if they all want to touch me, I see John glare at me. He doesn't like this, does he?

When the last of the people file out of the hall, I notice John talking to members of the council. They shoot me glances. I want to go back home. Rest with Genevine and Rusty, find out more about Rusty's life. Somewhere, deep down in my brain, the desire to find out what happened to cause this entire mess, The Fall, creeps up again.

Another look from John, and I know I'm being talked about. There's no way I can leave now. A family I don't recognize, thanks me for what I've done. I smile and embrace the man, and the woman. In the crowd that's milling outside I see Samantha. She looks over at me, and her eyes don't even register me. I feel a tinge of sadness. Don't think on her, I say to myself. You have so much more in your place. But first I have to head off whatever trouble is brewing with John and the council. I walk over.

"Tom," John says and reaches an arm out to me. "Come, the council wants to extend their gratitude for your bravery."

The men of the council look at me. I realize that I need to understand what their roles are. I recognize their faces, but nothing else.

They thank me then, as if they were ordered, walked out of the main hall. It's just John and me. The last council member leaves and the hum of the crowd drifting off outside fills the main hall.

"Care to join me?" John asks.

"Of course," I say. We head over to his place. Even though I'm sure that I'm too much of a hero to be touched, I glance over my shoulder. There's still a chance that John's glances my way mean he aims to get rid of me. I can smell the distinct stench of wood burning in the air.

Inside his place, he pulls out a bottle of whiskey. "You want some?"

I shake my head. "I'll be fine for now," I say. The last thing I need is alcohol swimming through me. Perhaps in front of someone like MacGee, but never in front of John. And why's that? Hasn't he been benevolent to you so far?

"Everyone's talking about how much of a hero you've turned out to be," John says.

"Well, whatever brings us closer to His Kingdom, right?"

John throws a dismissive glance at me. "And they're willing to forget the whole MacGee scenario."

I step forward to him. "I told you what happened."

John raises his hand. "It's not me you have to worry about, it's the council."

There's something in John's tone that tells me he doesn't believe me.

John pours himself a glass and takes a sip. "Some of the finest things in life. We had a few things right before the fall."

"That's true," I say. What does he want?

"How's the girl? What's her name?"

"She's fine." I wonder if telling John the girl's name will affect her treatment. Perhaps I could change it to something more palatable. "Rusty."

John cocks his head. "What?"

"Her name. It's Rusty."

He furrows his forehead. "What a name. No wonder they were struck down by God's hand."

I want to argue. I don't. Nor do I want to agree. That would only give John the impetus to change it. For some reason there's nothing I would want less. That name, the reaction on John's face, is what I need. "Perhaps God sent her to us," I say, hoping.

John pauses. "Perhaps."

"We should look to expand the flock where ever we can, isn't that right?"

"Well… Maybe, maybe not."

"Why not?" I ask.

"Our crops aren't working out."

"How come?"

"They just aren't. We might not be able to feed everyone as it is…" John says this while tilting his head at me. He narrows his eyes. "Then you go and invite a girl to come live with us."

"And?"

"Well the council doesn't like such behavior."

The air around me starts to thin out, and I feel light-headed. I'm staring into John's eyes, so I don't dare look over my back, but I'm expecting there to be guards. Did I lock the door behind me?

"My behavior?" I say, my vocal chords stretching, almost refusing to work. Aren't I a hero? And even though I had a premonition of evil creeping around, of too many eyes rolling my way, I always assumed it was because my nerves were still wretched after Jenny and MacGee.

"That's right," John says, his voice vibrating through his chest. There's a shine of amusement in his eyes. "They've been talking about this latest... transgression."

And all of a sudden I realize how precarious my situation is. Has always been, but it's only when you realize it that it stings. When you realize that your neck's on the line. "Me?... John you know—"

He raises his hand to stop me. I can see he enjoys this, but I have no time to confront that. "Tom, you know you don't have to explain anything to me, right?"

Of course, I'm not sure. "Right."

"But with this extra girl you just might have put us over the top. We need food, and we don't need extra mouths to feed."

What can I say?

"So no more? Next time you find one either get rid of her, or pass her on to the boys."

Pass her on to the boys? What does that mean? I'm sure that girl would have been raped if I hadn't spoken. Jim's words come back to me. Perhaps he was right about John. "Fine, it won't happen again."

John nods. "We have bigger problems too."

"Other groups we need to fight?"

"Well," John says with a dismissive wave of his hand. "That will always be around. I'm talking about our food and possible lack of children."

I must be giving off a confused look because I'm not sure how that works. "I thought too many people was our problem..."

"That girl was a problem, John. She wasn't one of us. She hasn't been vetted yet."

51

I'd completely forgotten about the trial. "She has to go through one? Isn't she too young?"

"You will be with her to vouch, but everyone has to."

John's words seem convoluted. "All right, she'll go through it. But there's still the issue of food. If we don't have enough why should we want more kids?"

"Tom, Tom, Tom," John says shaking his head. "You know what the Bible says. Go forth and multiply, right?"

"All right, but what about the food? We can worry about multiplying later."

"Why do you think people survive, Tom? Especially in this world where one look around gives you nothing to fight for."

I dig through my mind trying to think of what went through my mind when I first found out about the world. I had a desire to survive. But why? Wasn't there a hope to rebuild, to fight on? Isn't that innate? I realize that nowhere in this explanation did I think of God. But of course God comes into this, doesn't He?

"I'm not sure," I say. "I think that there are a few reasons. God for one."

"Of course God. But people are still of flesh. We all are. And we need reasons. If people can't prepare the world for their children, for the next generation, what else do they have?" John clasps his hands together. "This is how you need to see things, Tom. The word of God: 'Be fruitful, multiply' and the knowledge of flesh. This is how we survive. If we don't have any children, then the will to survive, to find new ways to get food, will soon wither away."

"But there are a few children," I say. I'm perturbed that Rusty doesn't figure in with this. Sure passing on your genes is important to everyone, but that doesn't mean that people have never adopted.

"We need more, Tom," John's voice booms.

I flinch.

"And so far there are none."

"None of our women have found a way to get pregnant."

"And is there a reason?"

"None so far. We think the radiation from the fall made either the men or women impotent."

I've had enough of this conversation. I don't like the shift of power that has just occurred. I am no longer the hero, but a child to be chastised for not seeing his ways.

"Then we'll find a way," I say. "God knows we're here. He let us survive, and He's testing us."

John looks exasperated, but eventually nods his head. "Yes He is."

I glance over at the map when it gets too quiet for my tastes. "How many more groups?"

"Three main ones. There might be more," John replies. He shakes himself out of his trance and walks to the map.

"We can find food from them," I say. I remember my cave, but I don't mention it. I only hope that Samantha and her man don't rat me out first.

"We could."

"That means that the flamethrowers are out," I say.

"That's right," John says. "I didn't think about that, but you're right." He nods his head thoughtfully.

I feel better now that there's a slight shift in the power between he and I.

"We need more scouts. More warriors. And we need to root out these bastards as fast as we can. We'll find food and we'll be fine," I say without really knowing if it will be that easy.

"That sounds good," he says, his voice betraying a certain amount of awe. "You really are a tough bastard, aren't you?"

"Kingdom of Heaven, right? We need to fight, and we need to do it hard."

"That's right."

"What time is the trial?" I ask.

"Tomorrow at noon."

We embrace. I walk out of his house, a weight lifted from my shoulders.

I enter my house. Rusty and Genevine are eating at the table. "She's still hungry?" I ask.

Genevine glares at me. "Your friend Samantha brought us some food. Or you some food," she says and points to the cookies.

I freeze. My face twitches as I wonder if Samantha is thinking about the cave full of food. I might need to head her off before she decides to talk.

Genevine sees my thoughts and mistakes them for something else. "What went on between you two?"

Now my heart jerks. "Us? What do you mean?"

"I mean," Genevine says, getting up from the table, a wary eye on Rusty. "I mean between you two."

"Don't be silly," I say. "I was a friend of her family."

"I've seen the look she gives you. That's not a friendly look," Genevine whispers into my ear. "But don't worry, I won't tell," she says. Her face is hard, but she playfully taps my cock.

I take a deep breath. "Did she want anything?"

"No," Genevine says.

"What about her," I say and point at Rusty. "How's she been?"

"She's behaving."

"She has a trial tomorrow at noon. We need to get her ready."

"A trial for her? She's only a child," Genevine says. "Are you certain?"

"Yes." I turn. "I need to go see what Samantha wants."

Genevine gives me a suspicious look. "Oh? Or is it something else you need to see?"

"I'll be back," I say and head out the door before Genevine can interpret anything else from my face.

It's getting chilly outside. I huddle inside my jacket. I'm not thrilled about having to find Samantha. I remember those moments alone with her, and try to scold myself for having ever made such a mistake. Instead of stifling my libido, my body shifts blood down there and Samantha's hips and waist appear in my mind. I'm filled with the delight of possibly pushing into her, the memories of those moments destabilize me.

With one hand I open my jacket and allow the cold to slap me out of my desires.

The sky is as dark and boding as ever and even though the cold is threatening to seep in, that I have others around me fills me with calm. A group of three young men walk by me. They slap my back and congratulate me. I smile back and shake their hands. "Get ready for more," I say. And they cheer and grunt. I walk further and take in the smells of different cooking wafting out from the various homes. It definitely doesn't seem like there's any food shortage, I think to myself.

That only gives me more reason not to mention the cave. I remember the cave when I shared it with Jenny; how I thought that it would be the base for a future of mankind. How foolish a thought that was. I stumble over a rock and keep walking. Had Jenny ever been happy with me? That thought, and my body's answer, in the form of melancholy, push down my spirits.

And I find myself in the same dark corner of the village. The houses, or shacks are vacant black hulls here, and only the smell of stagnant air meets my nose. MacGee was staying here but a few days ago.

So what? I force myself to think. As if his ghost is inside screaming my name, I walk away, trotting as fast as I can until I am near the populated houses, where the smells and noise of conversation calms me.

Around a corner I see a group of women, and as they walk by me, I see Samantha. She stops in her tracks.

"Tom, how nice to see you," she says, her voice is so sweet as to border on mocking.

"Hi Samantha," I say. "You wanted to see me?"

"I did," she says and takes my hand, pulling herself into an embrace with me. I grow larger, as I press against her breasts.

"I'll see ya'll later," she says to the three other women. The women walk by me, congratulating me on my heroism and flashing eyes that scream "we know".

When they're out of sight, and their chatter drifts into nothing, I grab Samantha by her forearm and bring her closer to me.

"What have you been telling them?" I ask, some spit flying out of my mouth.

She arches back. "Nothing."

"Don't lie. Why were they looking at me like that?" I dial back my anger, as I realize that I'll need her to be quiet about the cave, and thus need her on my side.

"I think you're crazy," she says.

I sigh. "Maybe. But you haven't told anyone anything, have you?"

"About what?" she asks. There is such innocence in that question that I'm slightly thrown off and wonder for a second whether I dreamed the whole thing.

"Nothing," I say. "Why have you been coming over to my place? Genevine will get suspicious."

"What are you talking about?" she asks with that same innocence.

I roll my eyes, but mainly because I'm nervous in the presence of such a dexterous feline.

"What did you want?" I ask.

"Why the past tense?"

I chuckle and she smiles. Even in the dark and only a sliver of a light from a shack, her smile pokes at my chest.

"Come on," I say.

"Can't I stop by and congratulate you? You *are* a friend of the family. And you should come by again."

I feel somewhat sheepish, as I think about her family, for accusing her of divulging the secret between us. I let a few seconds pass as I enjoy her smell, still sweet, still an aphrodisiac.

"By the way," I say. "Have you told anyone about the cave?"

"No. Why?"

"Don't. For now."

She pauses for a second, tilting her head as if she's weighing the pros and cons. "Okay."

"Thanks. And anyone else in your family, for that matter."

"Uh-huh. Anything else, boss?"

I smile. I actually feel proud to be called that. "Nope. I'll see you around, and I'll let you know when I can do dinner."

I turn and feel a tug on my hand. When I spin back, her face is only a few inches away from mine. I want to pull away, but my muscles are revolting and pushing towards her.

"And don't let him be a stranger either," she says and taps my cock.

Before I can even sniff some more of her, she's gone. I stand there, trying to come to grips with what has just happened. As my blood and muscles wind down, cry even, from the potential of another tryst, I blow a kiss into the wind.

Back at my house, Genevine and Rusty are still sitting around the table.

"Any food left?" I ask.

"Better make it yourself if you think you can wander off to find other women," Genevine says.

Her face is full of fire, and she stares at me like she's ready to slit my throat. Rusty gives me the same look, though it melts into a friendly grin after a few seconds.

I don't argue, after all I was just thinking about Samantha's insides, so I fish for a few pieces of bread and decide to chew that.

"You're going to have a trial tomorrow," I say to Rusty when I'm finished eating.

Rusty seems confused. "A trial?"

Genevine pats her arm in a slow rhythmic manner.

"Yeah, they're going to ask you some questions. You need to answer them right."

"Correctly?" Rusty asks or maybe tells me.

"You believe in the Lord, our savior?"

Rusty has an incredulous look on her face. "You're them."

Genevine doesn't seem to have the slightest clue.

"What do you mean?" I ask.

"I was always told about you crazies. And you're them."

I pause. There's something of MacGee in this child, so I don't cut her down, but she needs to know what to say or else I'm certain that John and the rest wouldn't think twice to treat her like MacGee or Thomas. "Who told you that?" I ask, thinking that she's talking about me.

"My family," she says, sticking out her face at me. She's been cleaned up and now a handful of scars are glowing on her face.

"Oh. About all of us?" I ask

"That's right."

I'm offended, but don't want to argue this point. I look at Genevine who seems to be nodding. "You agree?"

"You have evidence proving otherwise?"

I shake my head. "That's great; she goes talking like that all over the village, and they'll tie her to a stake."

Genevine doesn't retort, and Rusty only stares at me like she doesn't really understand the issue.

I crouch down to her. "You know that we're here to help you, right?"

She doesn't reply.

"I will help you all I can. But there isn't much choice here. Not for you. One day, maybe. But right now you're going to have to do as we say."

"Why?"

"There are people out there who don't want you here. They will be more than willing to have you slip up just so that they kill you. Do you understand?"

I look at her face. The corner of her mouth twitches. The beginnings of a cry. I grab her shoulders. "You do understand, don't you?"

She shudders and tears come out. All that toughness was just a front. She's been through so much, and here I am making it worse. I hug her, hold her tight. Genevine gives me a dirty look.

"I'm sorry," I say. I'm not thinking about John, or the Kingdom. I'm not even thinking, really. My heart's floating above MacGee, and Jenny. And maybe Carol, though I'm not sure. And mainly it wants to tell this little girl that I'll help her do anything, if only it will fill her with something other than tears.

"Don't worry, it'll be all right. You just have to lie until you're grown up. Then you can do what you want. If you want to get those who killed your family, I'll help you. Even if it's me. But you have to grow up a little. All right?" I say.

She stops crying. I kiss her forehead. She doesn't seem so sad, though that may just be something I want to see.

I make her promise not to say anything about crazies. Then I talk her through what she has to say tomorrow.

At night we let her sleep in our bed. She's twitching and asleep before I know it. Genevine has been quiet since Rusty cried. I assume it's because she's mad at me.

"What is it?" I whisper when Genevine is cold to my touch.

"Nothing."

It's too dark to see her face. I can smell her breath. Cumin, old, bad even, but I get closer to her so I can hear her better. Smell her skin. Feel her warmth.

"Is it because I made her cry?" I ask.

"No."

I can here her moving her tongue. She must be thinking. She leans in further to speak to me.

"I think what you told her…"

I can feel her warm breath on my ear lobe.

"Was great," she says. Her hand reaches around and squeezes me on my shoulder, before heading down and rubbing my stomach.

I remain still. My mind wanders over to what Rusty is doing, but a slight snore reminds me that she's had a full day. Genevine rubs me again, but instead of being sensual I feel ticklish. I dare not move away from her, though.

"Did you really mean what you said?" she asks.

"About getting back at us?"

"Even you." She stops rubbing.

For a few seconds I take in her breaths, punctuated by Rusty's snores, and the echo of the in between-silence off the walls. "I meant it," I say. "She has that right, don't you think?"

Genevine doesn't answer. Her warm breath lifts off from my face as she changes her body position to face the ceiling.

"Whatever you say," she says.

"Don't talk about this to anyone," I say. I want to make sure of that. Even if she doesn't agree with Rusty's rights.

"Of course not," she says, almost too loudly because Rusty stops snoring and moves.

We both hold our breaths until we hear Rusty return to her deep breaths and slight snores.

Genevine turns her head to me. "What kind of woman do you take me for?"

"I was just making sure," I say.

Soon the silence and the darkness seep into my mind and I float, clutching at sleep.

Genevine taps me and jerks me awake.

"What?" I ask, annoyed.

"We need to get married. People are talking. They know we're sleeping in the same house alone. It won't stand."

Half asleep, my mind snaps out of its stupor. "Marriage?" I ask. All the sensibilities inside me are saying no, you barely know her. Yet this isn't the world from before. And Genevine seems like a smart woman.

"Yes," she says.

And she knows these few secrets. So why not make it official?

"Sure. I mean. Yes."

"If you're not sure," she says, and I can hear her prop her head on her hand.

"I am," I say. She sounds hurt, as if she expected more enthusiasm. Reaching over, I pull her closer to me. "I am."

"Okay," she says. Though I'm not sure if she's happy or has given up. "We'll have to do it right after the trial. You have to ask permission from the council."

I pause. "Permission." This I don't like.

"Just put up with it for one day, okay?"

"Fine."

The trial with Rusty goes well. She's a natural liar and doesn't have to look up to me. The ceremony for the marriage lasts only a few minutes. Asking the council for permission is only a formality, though it still grinds against my ego. Genevine seems elated with the whole affair. John provides us with a pair of rings. Both made of scuffed steel. I kiss Genevine and tell her I have to work, and that she should take care of Rusty. I walk away before I can see her reaction.

I find Jim and head out with the scouts. I feel a flood of hope coursing through my veins, and I also want to watch the world go by me. It's the same landscape as before, that expanse of brown nothingness that at one point had threatened to eat me, but now it's a picture that I can examine, enjoy. There's meaning to all this.

"Heard you got married," Jim says and punches me. "Why'd you go and do that? I heard you had a good deal as it was."

The truck cab breaks out into laughter. I'm in the back with Jim. Mitt's driving, and Craig's in front of me.

I let out a disgruntled tsk. I think on Genevine's look when I walked away from her bordered on exasperated. She might even be thinking that I'm not enthusiastic about the wedding. I am, though.

"Well?" Jim asks, leaning into me.

"Why not?" I say. "She's a good woman, isn't she?"

"If she's such a good woman, how come you're here with us?" Mitt asks.

There is no answer for that one. I try to roll Genevine's image in my head. Or not so much her image as the chemical process with which she inhabits my mind. That means her smell, her touch, the beat of her heart, and how I react to it is in my head. Do I love her?

"No answer?" Jim asks and laughs, the other two join in. I have a feeling this might go on forever.

"Yeah, it doesn't take that long to figure out," Craig says. "I mean she's not bad looking, but why do you hate her?"

"I don't hate her," I say, and as soon as the words are out I wish them back because from the looks on their faces I can tell that I've risen to the bait. "I'm just out here for work."

They scoff. "Away for three days after you just got married?" Jim asks, this time his voice seems serious.

"Three days?" I ask. "I thought this was only for a day."

"No bud. This one's way too far away for that. We're spending a few nights out here," says Jim.

Now I wonder about Genevine, and how I wish to be in her arms. Silly me. "What are we checking out?" I ask, hoping to change the subject.

"The big three," Jim says.

"Big three?"

"These bastards are too big to trifle with, at least not now, so our job is to figure out a way to pick them off, one by one." Jim shifts in his seat, his hands slashing to pantomime the death he plans to dish out.

John never told me anything about this. "You mean they're made of more people than us?" I ask.

"Smart man," Craig says. "Isn't he smart?"

Everyone chuckles.

"Have they met each other yet?" I ask, wondering what would happen when alliances are formed.

"No. We're the only ones with vehicles, as far as we know, so it would take too long, to reach each other," Jim says with a measured gesture of his hands.

"That's good," I say. "But you think they're too strong for us?"

"Doesn't matter," Jim replies. "We're going to have to take them on." He squints at me. "Hasn't John told you this already?"

"No," I reply, wondering if that takes my stature in their eyes down a notch. What does it mean that John hasn't told me? It seems like he's taken me in his confidence. "When did he tell you this?"

"There's a meeting once a week. Military meeting. All the unit leaders, John and the council attend it." Jim finishes speaking and tsks as if this meeting is a hindrance.

"Basically," Mitt chimes in. "John tells us what we are about to do and the council agrees."

Jim shakes his head.

"And does anyone ever disagree?" I ask. I can see Jim disagreeing with everyone and everything he doesn't like.

"No way," Mitt says. "People used to disagree and argue all the time. But that was before the fall."

Jim nods in a reminiscent manner.

"And what happened after?" I ask.

"First week people were scared, though they still argued at the meetings. Then when all forms of communication stayed down, when John was certain that there weren't any other poor bastards in the world, he started to clamp down."

Jim grunts in agreement. "I don't like the bastard, but he's smart and knows what he's doing," Jim says. "He claimed something like emergency powers. Said it had to be done."

Mitt chuckled. "Even Jim's scared of him. Used to be the loudest one to shout him down, now he keeps quiet."

Jim looks off at his window. "Fuck off," he grumbles.

"Is that right?" I say, hoping to chide him in return for what he slung my way a few moments ago.

Jim shakes his head.

"This," Mitt goes on. "Is the only place you can talk freely." He waves his hand at his other two cohorts. "Anywhere else, and you're liable to get struck down."

I don't like that there's a schism in the group, but I'm glad to be included in it. "People have been ratted out?" I ask.

"Yeah," Jim says, swinging his head at me, his eyes burning. "The council used to be twice as big. When John claimed emergency powers, by way of the situation and what rights God bestowed on him, and this country..." He says the last word with a hint of irony. "Some people in the council started to complain. The ones who did it to his face were executed on the spot for trying to start a rebellion."

"Christ," I say, though I'm not sure what to think. Perhaps John did see something that needed to be squashed. Should I judge? Wasn't that more or less what I did? Cleared out my area of those who disagreed?

"Exactly," Jim says. "He found those out. Then he thinned out a few more when some people were called out for complaining outside the meetings. Shot them dead." He shakes his head.

"And no one said anything?" I ask, half trying to ask Jim why he would stay silent.

"No. I suppose we agreed to a level. You do have to keep the peace during such times. That's what the Constitution said, right?"

I nod. Of course, I'm not really thinking about whether what John did was right or wrong. What I'm thinking about is whether there is a reason John didn't invite me to those military meetings, and whether this means he sees me as an enemy. If so I'm in danger.

"Don't worry," Jim says and pats my lap.

"I'm not. I'm sure he had his reasons," I retort, perhaps a little too quickly to seem calm.

"I'm not talking about that," Jim says. The other two stay quiet in a way that makes me think they know what Jim is talking about. Am I that transparent? If so, I might be in more trouble than I think. I hold my handgun and stroke the slide.

"And now he doesn't shoot them," Craig says. "He has his courts to do that."

I feel anger directed at me. No one says anything else.

We drive for half a day and stop the car between some rocks near jagged hills. The hills are like smooth fingers reaching out to the sky. For some reason I'm thinking about a postcard I once saw from an old friend of mine. He had been hiking alone for months. What state was he in? The hills he showed looked just like this one. And he'd talked about how amazing it was. He'd been mesmerized with what he'd seen in the rocks. Said something about a timeless entity that would outlast all of us.

I reach for an overhanging rock and feel the texture of the rock. It's orange. There are lines. I forget what that means. Perhaps something to do with the ages with which it was layered? Millions of years, I think. Before man was man. And now it would be here long after we were. Sadness drifts down from my head to my body, and I feel like crawling up in a corner and dying. The thought grips me and freezes me.

Jim slaps my back, and I snap out of my melancholy.

"You all right?" he asks, eyeing me with worry.

"I'm fine. Just thinking something random," I say.

"Of the old times. Before the fall?"

"That's right," I say.

"Better not. It'll fuck with your head. Make you lose all hope."

"Well, there's always God to help us through, right?"

Jim spits on the ground in front of my shoes. Is he trying to say something?

"Christ, just when I think you're…" he trails off and looks at the other two scouts who are placing a camouflage net over the truck. "We're going to walk a long ways from here. Better get suited up," he says.

He seems so certain of his station in life, and yet there's a bubbling anger about him. Like he wants to change the world to what his mind has always seen it as.

"You don't think much of John, do you?" I ask.

He examines my face, looking for something to supplement the words. "He's smart. I'll give him that much."

My mind flinches. Was that asking too much? I think about the men that John killed on the basis of whispers. I freeze again, but this time it's fear. I want to ask him about MacGee but decide to stay away. I'm just too willing to open up, I think. If Jim watched John execute those men, then perhaps Jim was on John's side.

"Why?" Jim asks.

"No reason," I say. "So what group are we going to check out?"

Jim's eyes run over me, and dart off to the landscape behind me, before coming back to me. "It's one of the first ones we saw when we started to scout the area. They seem like a decent lot, but we're not sure. And," he says and shrugs. "They're sitting on food, so we have to figure out a way to get to them. That's what this is all about."

"And the women!" Mitt says. I glance up. I wasn't aware that the two of them were listening in on us.

"Women?" I ask.

"Yeah, you know about our pregnancy problem, don't you?" Jim says.

"I do, but why do we care about women?"

"See if any are pregnant and bring them in."

"Are you serious?" I ask.

"Of course, why wouldn't I be?"

"But we need food."

"And? Your friend John believes in the be fruitful and multiply part of the Bible, and we're going do just that."

Jim's voice is tinged with irony.

I let out air and nod, trying to seem as grave as possible.

"Let's go sweethearts," Craig yells. The two of them have backpacks and are moving on out. "Or if you want to blow him, Jim, we'll wait around the corner."

Jim spins with such ferocity that I jump back.

"You listen to me, you little fuck, one more smart ass remark and I'll come over there and stick my hand so far up your ass, you won't be able to stand for weeks. You get me?"

Craig even seems taken aback. "All right, Jim, Christ." He and Mitt turn and start walking, mumbling amongst themselves.

"Easy," I whisper. I don't like it when Jim acts out of control.

He turns back to me with a grin and wink. "Sometimes you have to keep the young lions at bay."

I smile. We grab our backpacks—Jim gives me one he has for emergency situations—and head out. It feels exceptionally heavy and immediately starts to dig into my shoulders and hips.

We stay some ways behind Mitt and Craig, clambering over rocks and walking on ledges. After an hour, we come to the base of a tall rock.

"We use this to look out," Jim says.

"Yeah," Craig says, his hurt tone from before completely gone. "Jim here is a fucking monkey. He can climb it, no ropes, nothing."

"Is that right?" I ask. "Bet I'm faster."

Jim laughs. "This ain't no ladder, Tom, leave it to me."

"Let's see," I say. "I'm sure I can beat you." I'm feeling a surge of energy as Jim shakes my hand. There's nothing I want more in this world than to crush him, put him in his place and feel them all look at me in awe. My mind, for a split second flashes to the moment I held that woman at gunpoint, when I shot Jenny's family, Jenny's squirming, when Samantha and Sarah held me in esteem, Samantha's gasps. And these flashes set of a chemical reaction and send more energy to my muscles.

I let Jim go ahead, then leap up on a rock and start my way up a crack. It takes me several hundred feet up. When it ends I lean into it and rest on my feet. The rock here is like sandpaper and my hands are ripped up. I stretch out my fingers. My forearms feel tired. Already? Surely I climbed more near Samantha and her family? But my muscles aren't listening, they're protesting and claiming that they'll soon quit. I glance at the waves of orange rocks around me. There are still a few hilltops blocking my view of the entire landscape, but what I see is beautiful. The entire land shivers in elongated shadows.

The cliff face looms above me and doesn't seem to end. My heart starts beating faster, and trembles. And soon I'm clutching on for dear life, not sure why I was so cocky.

Jim's head appears below me. He's following the same crack. "Hey old man!" I yell. Why don't you find your own routes?"

He stops and cranes his neck back and forth, his eyes darting back and forth. They stop when they rest on my waving hand.

He positions himself on his feet and points at me with one hand. "You young prick. I climbed this thing long before you ever did. Get off *my* route."

It really is hard to tell if he's joking or not.

"You're kind of behind," I say, half chuckling to myself. "Why don't you quit while you're ahead?"

"Fuck you," Jim says, and as he does a small cloud of spittle flies through the air. "I know why you stopped. Your hands are getting cut up, aren't they?" He lets out a forced laugh and looks down as if the other two scouts can hear him. "Well, sweetheart, don't let this be your place of rest." He hooks his hands back in the crack and starts his way up to me.

Though his last comment strikes a little too close to my fears, I'm still elevated from mocking him. A few shakes of my hand, and I look for divots to stick my fingers in. I see a few and lean to my right as far as I can. I hook in with two fingers and pull myself up. I keep my head up and looking for holds. My muscles are tired, but I push past that. This will not be my resting place.

Hold after hold and soon I find myself on a flatter curve of the rock. It's flat enough that I can rest myself on the holds, but it's still steep enough that if I let go I won't be able to climb up on my own power, and though I won't fall immediately, I will sooner or later get tired and, as always, gravity will win.

And then the holds run out.

I grasp the last ones I'm holding on to. It's an excuse to rest. The day is winding down. I wonder what I'll do. I glance below to see if Jim is anywhere to be seen. He isn't. Relax. Look for something to hold. There's always something. I look. Nothing. I push myself from the rock and, gripping the holds like the lifelines they are, I see nothing. I head back down. The slope makes it hard. I go down almost a hundred feet before I see something.

"Hey, princess."

It's Jim and he's above me, on a part of the rock that's steep.

"You took the false route, didn't you?" he says and shakes his head. "Rookie move. You have to come this way. But. Find your own route."

"Bastard." And I see the route he's taken and follow it. No time for another, I have to get to the top before him.

I work my way from hold to hold. Soon I'm only a few feet behind him.

"Get your own route," he says and spits at me.

It lands right on my forehead. "You fucker," I say. He giggles and keeps climbing.

My muscles are reacting slowly now, screaming really, and though I look for another route, there's none to be seen.

I make it to the top with hardly anything left in my reserves. I haven't brought food, and I'm exhausted. Jim lends me a hand to get me to the table top.

"Beautiful view, eh?" he asks.

Catching my breath, my hands on my knees, I take a look. It is gorgeous. The curvature of the earth rushes away from me and the small waves of nearby hilltops cede to a flat expanse punctuated with hills here and there. They're like cities, these small ranges of hills. The sky isn't as gray, and in fact seems neither cloudless, nor cloudy. Jim is looking through his binoculars. "They're still there," he says.

"The group?"

"That's right. They're all huddled up. I wonder why."

I sit down. I could sleep forever. "You have any food?"

"Are you serious? A young man like you is wiped out?"

He has a look on his face that says he's down to chide me, so I stay quiet.

"Not like that small hill you climbed where we found your lot, is it?"

I hold my breath. He was the one that first saw us? Then did he see everything? Does he know about Samantha? "You saw us first?" I ask.

He lowers his binoculars. "That's right. Us three. Saw you on a random chance. We were on foot back then, and Mitt raises his binos to see what was around, and he sees you half way up that rock."

I picture them seeing me and feel a tinge of pride. But that doesn't last long. My mind is swimming in the past now and I can't stop it. The thoughts bounce from the looks of awe Samantha gave me to the conversations I had with MacGee. Then it rests on the fact that if I hadn't been a show off, they would never have found me, and MacGee would be alive today. But would I have met MacGee then? He would still be alive. But I had to see MacGee to bring him over to us, to find a friend. Sadness envelops me.

"Come back, Tom," Jim says and sits next to me.

That's why I like him. There's a lot of MacGee in him. "I'm here."

"You're carrying a lot of crosses, aren't you?"

How do I answer that? Try to find out something that matters, my mind shouts.

"How long did you observe us for?"

"A day. Then we went back and got the others."

"Were you going to kill us?"

"No," Jim says.

I don't believe him.

"Come on," I say.

"No, really. The biggest thing was that you were believers."

"So how come we don't ask that anymore?"

Jim shrugs. "The food thing kinda puts a hiatus on matters of expansion."

I let out air. There's no use arguing this. "What did you see when you observed us?" I ask.

He looks at me and smiles. "You have secrets, Tom?"

"Tell me, what?"

"Not much. You guys were working on that weird shrine. I think ya'll were drinking, right?"

"That's all?"

"Why, is there more?"

"No," I say and sit up straight. That urge to open up is banging against my heart. Should I? I'm being foolish. I'm married now, which means that I'm more than ever a part of this whole group. I may not agree with some things but that's the way a society works. "Are we heading back soon?"

"We will," Jim says.

"What did you do before the fall?"

Jim shakes his head. "Was a truck driver. Then I fell in with John and his group. He was a good man and helped out people in his flock whenever he could."

He used 'was' to describe John.

"You have a wife and family?"

"Yeah, one son. They were in Portland when it all happened. Buying supplies for us." He shakes his head, staring ahead.

"My wife was in Portland when it happened too. Or at least I think so."

I feel his eyes on me, but I stare ahead at the punctuated horizon.

"Damn shame, isn't it?" he says.

"I know. Never expected it, though now that you think about it, it makes perfect sense."

"Only now," he says, his voice low and rusted.

"My wife was in Portland too," I add.

A stillness envelops us both.

"I heard your story about the cave," he finally says.

The cave. The past life where I could spend weekends exploring caves just because it was fun. My mind flies to the moment where I saw the crater that was Portland, the moment I knew looking for my wife would be a useless endeavor, assuming she survived. I remember sitting there, the pit of despair in my body, and how that family tried to sneak up on me. Anger at the under-handed manner of the family fills me.

"What do you make of it?" I ask.

He shrugs.

"Did you go to Portland after the fall to see the remains?" I ask.

"Not for a while. And what we saw was nothing. Just a crater. Dead bodies under ash, if you could make any out."

"John mentioned that there were a lot of straggling survivors. You find any there?"

"I suppose we found some, but they were all in pretty bad shape and a far ways away from Portland. I think the cities got it the worst."

"You killed those you found?" I ask.

Jim shifts his arms and looks at his hands. "We had to. Trust me. Most of them were close to death and beyond medical care."

The wind picks up, as if it's trying to say something. I know trying to wonder if one of the people they shot was Carol is a bad route of thoughts. There would be no way of ever knowing.

"I'm not sure if I was the lucky one," I say. "Never knew what happened to my wife, and guess I never will."

"I'm with you," Jim says. "Don't repeat this in front of anyone else, but I don't see us surviving as lucky."

"What do you see it as?"

"Punishment."

"For what?"

He doesn't answer.

What does he mean? Is Jim more like MacGee than I ever expected? "You think God is punishing us?" I ask.

Jim scoffs and looks at me, before turning back to the horizon.

The silence grows, whines in my ear. Jim doesn't move, almost like he's holding his breath. He must have strong doubts about everything. Is that a good thing? Wasn't that what killed MacGee and Jenny? Didn't it almost kill me? If I hadn't found a strength of purpose in surviving, in pushing God's Kingdom, what would I have done? Would I even be alive?

And at that moment, the whine of nothing taking over my mind, I stare out at the horizon and see a combination of lit up orange clouds that forces me to close my eyes. The wind picks up. My heart beats faster. A warmth spreads through my body and I wonder what this sensation, something I never felt before, is. I've made it this far. What a pleasant surprise. And soon I feel at peace, and I feel sorry for Jim.

"You sleeping?" Jim asks after a while.

I open my eyes; the sky is the same. I take a deep breath and smell the ground, something more than the sterile nothing that was prevalent when I first saw this dead landscape. "No." My insides are still at peace, though the trigger—whatever it was—is gone.

"You look out of it."

I examine the lines on his face. He's old and tired. "You should have more hope," I say.

His face scowls, the lines spread and curve. "What the hell's gotten into you?"

"I'm just saying."

"Oh right. Because you got lucky a few times you feel like you know it all, right?"

I know he's baiting me so I don't reply.

"And you think you can act better than others, like your friend John."

The name John hits me, and I realize that I don't like it when Jim puts John down.

"I don't."

Jim gets up. "It's time to head back and do the Lord's work."

He doesn't sound sarcastic.

"Yes, let's," I say.

When we get back down the sun has fallen into the horizon and the sky is already burning.

"What took you two so long?" Craig asks, a smirk on his and Mitt's face. "Who was the catcher?"

Jim punches him in the shoulder. There's a crunching sound and Craig's face flinches, though he then pretends to laugh it off.

"You two recon the area?"

Mitt and Craig look at each other like scolded children.

"Christ," Jim says. "Do I have to do everything myself here?"

"Stay here." Jim walks off.

After he's gone I look at Mitt and Craig. They're staring at the ground in front of them.

"Something the matter with you two?" I ask.

"No," Mitt says. "Jim just gets too angry too quick."

"I know," Craig jumps in. "I think he needs to watch it."

"What do you mean?" I ask. "He means well."

"Oh," Craig says. "We know that. We're like family. But if he lets all this get to him, he's not going to be liked by the council."

"Or John," Mitt says.

"You'd think he'd know better," Craig says.

"Why's that?" I ask.

"He used to be a soldier."

"Jim?" I ask.

"Yeah. Real survivor. That's why he's the head of all military ops for us."

This seems to make sense. "He's survived this long..." I say, though I can't finish the thought. That's what he meant when we talked at the top of the mountain. He meant that he had been lucky too and seen that luck run out.

"He'll be fine," Mitt says.

"Where did he go?"

"It's getting dark. So no lights, just incase they see us. So he's going to make sure there's not a better place to sleep for the night."

The shadows of the surrounding hills are bearing down on us. The air is chillier than ever and a shiver runs up my body. I would like a fireplace, something like we had with MacGee and Samantha's family.

"Did you two remember when you snuck up on us?" I ask.

They're shuffling through their backpacks and they give me an odd look. "What do you mean? Just now?" Mitt asks.

"No. When you found me and Samantha and MacGee. Before we joined the group."

They exchange smirks.

"Oh that," Craig says. "We didn't see much. Why do you ask? Sounds like you have a secret."

Are they playing with me? "What did you end up telling John and the council about what you saw?" I ask.

"Nothing," Mitt says. "That there was a family that would be easy to overwhelm."

That's an odd thought: that I was looked upon as an easy victim.

They don't seem to like my reaction and go back to their backpacks. "You should pull out a sleeping bag. Tomorrow we'll walk up early."

Jim comes back. No one greets him and he pulls out his sleeping bag and rolls into it.

In my backpack I find a sleeping bag and hop into it. The shadows have spread everywhere and the sky is dark, with only a hint of light reflecting off it. I'm tired, and I'm still not sure what to make of Jim. I pissed him off, yet I still want to befriend him.

My mind drifts off to Genevine. I shouldn't have left, but there was a call deep inside my bones to take off. How could I have disagreed with that? I can only hope that she's thinking about me at this moment. Hopefully in a less than angry manner. It was a good idea to marry her. We've shared so much. And when I lie down to her I can feel so close to her that it shifts my perception of space.

I think of Jenny and how we rarely got along after *that night.* And how she still means so much to me. My heart caves in and sadness erupts through my bones. Think of something else, not that moment with Jenny on that cliff. You have Genevine now. You found inner peace, purpose. Surely that was God talking to you, right? God. I gulp. Would He forgive me? Surely letting me get this far was a sign. And hadn't I acted like the good Samaritan when I saved Rusty?

The moon lights up the back of clouds and the wind picks up, howling through the gaps in the rocks. One of the others shuffles, and I turn my head to look. I can see all three lying in a row, trying to stay together for warmth. I shift over until I'm next to one of them. The cold has already pierced my bag and is working its way to my skin.

Just the knowledge that we could be ambushed and killed sends another shiver through me. How I used to like camping. I should have spent more time doing it with Carol. Perhaps if I had done so we could've died together. But that was before all this, a voice in my head shouts. Stop looking back. You have this opportunity and you need to take it. There was a God in all of this, wasn't there? I look around. Alone amongst the rocks. My mind's eye zooms out to the world, or a picture I'd seen of it. Give me a signal I dare, or maybe ask.

The wind picks up, and I feel it sting my face. It howls between the rocks and it fills my head and my chest with the knowledge that I am answered. Calm, I fall asleep.

I wake up when it's still dark. I hear shuffling. I look over and there's someone next to me. I hear more shuffling. I turn again, trying to make it appear like I'm doing so in my sleep. There's the outline of a man several feet over. He's staring at the ground in front of him. Have we been found out? I reach for my pistol, tucked away in my pants. My mouth's dry. I can try and wake up the person next to me, but there's always the chance that they'll be too loud. I grip the pistol grip and place my finger on the trigger. Maybe it's the group we're trying to recon. Maybe they've sent out a scout. Could be that they saw us on top of that mountain?

The man stomps his feet a few times, mumbles and walks over to us. I strain my eyes, making sure not to move my head, to see if he has anyone else with him. Should I let him come any closer? Should I blast him right now? The man stoops over and rolls into a sleeping bag. Was that Jim? He shuffles in his bag and shifts over. A few minutes later I hear loud snoring. Mitt and Craig move and soon they're all breathing together. I keep my eyes open for a few seconds before I fall asleep.

"Rise and shine."

I open my eyes. Jim's face is blocking half my view. The sky behind him is dark, though it has enough light that the outlines of the rock tops can be seen clearly.

"You were sleepwalking," I say to him. I see that the other two haven't woken up yet. Their heavy breathing only makes me want to sleep even more.

He shakes his head. "No I wasn't."

I sit up. "Yes you were."

"You ready for this?" he asks.

"What are we doing today?" I say, letting him get away with the change of subject.

"We're going to see if we can cull these bastards."

I hope there're no children.

"What do we know about them?" I ask.

"They're some vicious bastards," Jim says.

"Why?"

"They own slaves, just like your girl Rusty's people."

"Really?"

"Yup. Full sale slaves. And they eat their own."

This seems a little much. "Are you sure?" I ask.

"You think I'm kidding?"

There's no way I can win this one. "You were sleepwalking."

"Well come and see, princess."

I nod to the other two. "What about them?"

"Don't worry, they'll be fine."

My bones creak and moan as I step out of my bag and pack my bag again.

"Leave it here," Jim says. In the darkness I'm almost certain that he's MacGee.

We walk for a few minutes, Jim leading the way. At his signal we fall to our bellies and crawl up a slightly inclined boulder. An insect crawls near my forearm, but when I look there's nothing there.

"There."

There's a fire at the bottom of a flat basin and figures moving around it. The basin is surrounded on all sides by towering rocks with black eyes, and it's only when I look closely do I see that they're in fact caves. I see shadows.

A stench rises to my nostrils. It's coming from the basin area, probably from the people. Can it be that they stink? No, it's something else. Something more decrepit, something more like death. I sense someone is watching us so I glance over my back. Nothing. Rocks. Shadows. If there is something or someone there I won't see them.

Jim leans in to me. "Don't worry. They don't send out scouts. Look there," he says and points to a corner.

There's a channel that leads into the dark.

"What?"

"They've water down that path. They usually go one by one. John's plan was to bleed them there until they were finished." He stops, and I can tell he expects me to say something about that.

"That's the plan?" I ask.

Jim shakes his head. "It's what your friend John said."

Doesn't seem like the best plan. Not for a large group. "How many are there?"

"Hundred at last count."

"How many women?"

"Fifty."

Jim is getting annoyed, so I stop.

Then a chant arises from the basin. The fire has grown and the people around it are chanting. It's a slow and simple chant. They're stomping their feet to a beat. And a cry goes out. I see three people emerge from one of the black holes. Two large men have someone small and hunched over between them. They drag the person to the fire. It's a man who looks to be in his fifties. Tied up. Jim hands me the binoculars.

The man's face is dark and he has tears streaming down. A groan leaks out of his mouth and tickles my insides.

The people from the fire, about ten of them, surround him. They're chanting louder now. It's in English, yet I can't make out the words. The man's hands are behind his back, and he's shaking his head. One of the people slaps him, and he barely maintains his balance.

The chant gets even louder. The mouths all across the rocks light up, and I see scores of shadows shaking in rhythm with the chant. It's loud enough now that it's shaking the very air I'm breathing, and though the man's mouth opens, I can't hear anything. He must be screaming for mercy. I steady my arms and try to see his eyes through the binos. I want to look away. Everything in my body wants to look away so badly, and yet my muscles won't listen.

An arm flashes out from the crowd around the man, and he falls over. An ax comes out. It's quick, a blur. Red paints the ground below the man. His mouth is open and between the chants a high-pitched scream echoes off the rocks. Something is snaking around my body, but I don't bother to see what it is. Instead I focus on the man's eyes. They're brown. Maybe black. What did he do to deserve such a fate?

Other people are behind him, and they are tying him to a log. The man is kicking and arching his back. More men step forward. They subdue the man with kicks. They've now chained him to the log. Only the man's head moves. He's snapping it back and forth with such ferocity that I'm surprised it doesn't come unhinged. Whatever's crawling up my skin has entered my body and is crawling, cold and mucous covered, down my cavity. I feel sick. And still I focus on the man's eyes.

His screams shake the basin. They frighten me, and feed the thing crawling around my heart and intestines. The crowd absorbs these screams and grows more energized. They're lifting the log. And now the man is in the flames. Writhing. Arching. I see his eyes and his mouth through the flames.

The crowd is cheering. They remove the blackened corpse from the fire. People come forward and chop at the charred remains. They take pieces of his arm and legs, then torso. The thing has tightened its grip around my belly. I feel nauseous. I put down the binoculars. The sky is breaking into dawn.

With Jim I slide back until we're out of view.

"That was horrible," I say.

Jim regards my comment with a grunt.

"They deserve what they get," I say. This is what John meant. He was right. There can be no agreement with such people.

Jim spits and scrunches one side of his face at me.

"Do they have guns?" I ask.

"No. Not that we've seen. Only axes." He hacks up phlegm and spits again. "You want to shoot 'em all for that? But there're lots of them, Tommy boy. We don't have the bullets to shoot them all."

"Nor can we kill them all at the watering hole," I say.

"Now you're thinking. So how do we do it?"

"Weren't you a soldier?"

"So?"

"How come you didn't mention it before?"

"I didn't feel like it."

That hurts. "And what did you learn when you were a soldier?" I ask.

"Not much. Mainly how to shoot. You don't learn things like this," he says and points to where the basin full of people lays.

"How about we kill a few at the watering hole and finish the rest with bullets?"

He laughs. A little too loudly for my tastes.

We head back to the other two. They're awake and sitting up in their bags. I realize that I'm hungry.

We eat small rations in a block form.

"So did you see their early morning ritual?" Mitt asks and winks at me.

"They do that every morning?" I ask.

"Of course, they've gotta eat, don't they?" Jim says.

Is he still angry?

"Another lovers' quarrel?" Craig asks and winks at Mitt.

Jim looks up and the two stop giggling.

"We need to stop these people," I say, my mind still festering on the man's eyes, etched into my mind.

"Oh look here. Tom's shocked at what they do," Jim says.

"Come on," Mitt says. "Even you have to admit they're barbaric."

Jim doesn't reply.

I decide that I've had enough of his attitude. He's acting like a child. And besides, though he had some tactical sense in the last battle, it was I who showed mettle when we were in that cave. So what if he was a soldier? Perhaps he's broken. Especially if he doesn't want to admit these people deserve a fate at the edge of a sword.

"What do you think of the plan to kill them at the watering hole," I ask Mitt and Craig. Jim gets up, stares at me, then stomps off.

"What got into him?" Mitt asks.

"I don't know, I thought you two would."

"No," Craig answers. "Never seen him this ornery before."

"And the plan?" I ask.

Craig shrugs. "Doesn't seem like much of one. I mean I suppose a person goes down there every few hours. But we'll get what, twenty per day?"

"No more," Mitt adds. "Unless we're here for some month long siege, we can't leak them out that way."

"But we can't face off with all of them at once."

They shake their heads.

"What about bombs?" I ask.

"You mean grenades?" Mitt asks.

"What about them? We have a few."

"Well we could," I say and pause, trying to act relaxed as I think of a plan. "Bring them out. There're a hundred of them, so we can cull them as we pull them out." I pause. I read this somewhere. It was done by the Mongolians as they tore across Eurasia; they would attack, feign retreat and pull the would be victors into a trap.

"And how do we do that, general?" Jim has returned from where ever he huffed off to and seems geared to argue with me.

"We kill them until they are forced to chase us. We have rifles, right?"

Mitt nods.

"We need to find the best avenues to have them chase us down. The first question is whether they know about this area or not. In other words have they explored it? If they have it won't work."

"They haven't. Not well, at least," Jim answers me, his eyes still blazing with contempt.

"Are you certain?" I ask.

"Of course. These hills are empty except for us, and there's no sign that anyone has been through here since the fall."

"How can you tell?" I ask. There doesn't seem to be a way to leave tracks on the rocks.

Jim laughs. It's forced, too heavy with the throat to be a proper laugh. The three of us shift our feet uncomfortably.

"Leave that to me," Jim says. His voice softens: "They only set up ambushes for stragglers on the plain area outside that basin. They never once hit the rocks here."

I dip my head.

"So we pull them out?" Mitt asks.

"We hit them in that watering hole, and we can snipe them. Then when they come after us, after we have hit their stronger people, we will let them give us chase of one of us. And pull them into a place we can trap them. We just have to find it."

Jim smiles at me with approval. "I already found several such places." He mock scoffs at me. "What would you ladies do without me?"

We follow him as he shows us a place that looks like an old riverbed that leads to an old pond bed. If I had any illusions that the plan was mine, Jim's thinking and specific ideas put that to rest. "We'll place a rope here. The fastest one amongst us," he says and points at me. "I'm talking to you, Tommy boy. That man will have these bastards chasing him. And you can't leave them in the dust. They have to think that they have you within their grasp. Otherwise if you get too far away, they'll get lost. We can't have that."

I'm not too happy about being bait, but I nod.

"You'll lead them here, and you'll have a few seconds to climb up the rope and cut it. We'll be here to help. But don't count on that, all right?"

"All right," I say, my voice almost a croak. I'm imagining myself running from these men. These men who ate a helpless old man. I know I'm stronger, and I'm doing something good, and that I've already proven myself, but the very idea is draining blood from my legs.

"Uh oh," Jim says. "Look at our big hero, he's scared."

"I'm not." I lie. Everything—Jim, Mitt, Craig, the rocks—morphs into ugly laughing faces with the eyes of the man who was grilled alive. Why am I acting so weak? Wasn't I brave in that cave? How's this different?

"We're going to have to set up some traps. Mitt, you have those stakes in your pack?" Jim asks, turning away from me.

"A few."

"We'll need them. Craig I'm going to need you to dig like your life depends on it. We'll try to get some sleep in the day. But tonight will be the time we strike. Slowly and one by one. Evening is when they hit the watering hole."

It sounds like a marvelous plan and yet my vision and thoughts are tunneling into one main idea: self-preservation. "How are we certain that they haven't explored these hills?"

"Of course we are, Tom. Don't go all weak-kneed on me just yet."

"How?"

"They worship these rocks. For some reason they have it in their heads that they are not to enter them."

I don't ask Jim how he knows this because in his words I find the strength returning to my legs. These people don't believe in God. No, they're heathens who believe in rocks, and eating people. And in that I know I'm right and that we'll persevere.

We all walk to the edge of the basin behind a rock where we're out of sight from the enemy's caves. I hear screams, though they could be screams of joy.

"Mitt, the stakes," Jim whispers. "We will use one of these per hole. Mitt, use your knife and sharpen them."

Mitt nods.

The strength that returned to my legs is losing out to an ambivalent yet strong feeling that evil is nearby. Perhaps the blood from that man turned loose a ghost on the soil around here. And I fear the men on the other side of the rock. I twist my hands and look at the lines formed as I cusp them. We shouldn't be talking so close to the enemy. As if to answer me, silence floats over the rock.

I tap Jim. He looks at me, more annoyed than ever. I smell something now. "I think we should leave."

He stares at me. I feel sand falling on my head, and I point up.

All three of us freeze. We crouch underneath the slight overhang of the rock. More sand falls in front of us. I feel my heart in my throat. All my strength's gone. After all I'd done, I was still scared of dying. We were trapped. I reach for my hand gun. Jim places a hand on my gun, stopping me. My hand is shaking; I hope he doesn't see that. I'm supposed to be a hero.

"Do you see anything?" A voice yells. It's right above us. I can smell something like grilled meat so close. My body's crumpling up. It takes all the energy I have just to stay still. I take a deep breath, though I have to hold it when Jim flashes me a look. Am I being too loud?

"No, nothing," another voice says. This one is not above us. I turn my head slightly. Now I smell us, and hope, pray that they don't smell it either. Rocks go flying out of our view.

"Still?"

"Nothing. Jay said he saw something on this rock."

"I know I heard someone talking."

They sound like little kids.

"All right," A louder deeper voice resonates. "Does anyone see anything?"

A chorus of no's goes up.

"Very well. We'll keep an eye out. Everyone back. These rocks can speak sometimes."

Silence falls. I miss the days when silence included the chirping of insects. Now it only means wind.

After a few seconds of the wind rubbing on rocks, I lean forward only half an inch.

Jim's hand reaches for my collar so quickly that it takes a second for me to realize that he's pulling me back. The ferocity in his eyes freezes me, and I hold my breath again.

We wait for what seems to be an eternity.

The wind stops. It's my beating heart that I hear now, feel expanding and contracting my arteries. I'm thinking about the time in the cave after Jenny had killed herself and how I felt the nothingness of the land and how that filled me with such dread. I thought I was going to die then. I thought the nothingness would eat me. Finish me. And now I feel the same even though there are people next to me.

And evil people on the other side of that rock. Was I evil when I did that to Jenny? How about MacGee? No, I try to tell myself, I wasn't. I wasn't like these people. In the end there was a difference: I will become a better person.

Just as my thoughts seem like they'll overwhelm me, I see sand slide down the rock. Footsteps walk away, or maybe I'm hoping that they are. We wait even longer.

Finally, Jim looks at Mitt and Craig and gives them a fist gesture. I was so busy just trying to join these scouts that I forgot that maybe they have a whole set of procedures amongst each other that I haven't bothered to learn.

Jim leans into me. "Can you smell anything?"

I take a deep breath, slowly rushing air past my nostrils. It's clean. But then again, I didn't notice that it was clean before, so maybe I'm missing something. We can't stay here. So I shake my head. My muscles tighten around my bones. I wonder if I'll be able to move.

"We move on my signal. You'll follow me."

Mitt and Craig step, and hook, out and point their weapons in opposite directions. They nod. Jim moves out in a straight line before spinning and pointing his weapon at the top of the rock we were just hiding under.

Though I'm not sure of where he wants me to go, I run so I'm behind him and look at where his weapon is pointed. No one's there. The tension in my muscles relaxes.

"Keep moving," Jim growls.

I run behind a rock and turn. I see Jim hold his position as the other two turn and run towards me. I have a good view of the top of the large rock we were hiding under. And when I see the movement of a head at the edge, my muscles freeze. I raise my pistol. It takes a second for me to realize that I'm holding my empty hand and that it's making some nonsensical gesture at Mitt and Craig.

Craig tilts his head as he jumps up over a rock. The look on his face is confusion. Perhaps he stops because he thinks I'm telling him to. But that doesn't really matter as I notice a red blotch on his shirt, with something protruding from it. On his way down, another blotch appears on his chest, and he collapses right next to me. Two arrows stick out of his back.

Mitt stumbles over Craig and hides behind the rock. Several arrows land on the rock we're behind as well as into Craig's body. Where are they firing from? I realize that the head is directing the fire of the arrows, who are safe behind the rock.

"Craig?" Mitt screams and pulls Craig by his hand behind the rock. He turns Craig over and a gurgling sounds emits from his chest. He doesn't move. Mitt places two fingers on Craig's wrist.

"He's dead," Mitt says. His face is drained of color.

A gunshot. Arrows cut through the air. I peek back over the top of the rock. Jim is firing at one of the heads peeking over the large rock.

"Run Jim!" I yell and fire at the head bobbing up and out of my view. Jim turns and runs to us. He gets behind the rock as several arrows fly through the air and whistle by me. I hear yells on the other side. It sounds like they're moving.

"We've got to keep going," Jim says as he adjusts his gun and puts in another clip. He's breathing hard. I've never seen him scared. "This was an ambush." His voice is surprised, even hurt.

I nod when he grabs my arm, his nails digging into my skin. Does he need my approval? More arrows fly over the rock. One skips over the top and, with its downwards trajectory, it flies right above my head. I flinch down, but it would have been too late. He looks over at Mitt.

"Did you hear me? We have to move now!"

"We're taking him," Mitt says, his eyes red, tears streak through the dirt on his cheeks, and his voice pierces the air with its fear.

"Is he alive?" Jim asks.

"No," Mitt says.

Jim takes a step over and grabs Craig's bag and his gun. Then all his ammunition.

Mitt grabs his arm. "What the hell are you doing?"

Jim breaks the hold with a twist of his arm and grabs Mitt by his collar. "We have to get out of here. We can't be weighed down by his corpse. Do you understand? Anyone falls they are left behind. And we have to get out now before they encircle us."

Mitt's face doesn't seem to comprehend this.

Jim shakes his head. "Ready?" he says to me.

I've melted to the ground, and I can't move one inch. I nod. I feel safe here behind the rock, but I know what Jim says makes sense. "Mitt," I start to say, but the croak that leaks from my lips doesn't do me any favors.

"On my count start shooting over the—"

Jim is cut off by a flurry of arrows that arc downwards and land almost vertically. They're firing straight up into the air, the bastards. One arrow lands directly into Craig's head, planting him firmly into the ground. Another scrapes my pants and just slices into my skin as it lands by my thigh. I shield my face with my arms, even though something in my head is saying that it's no use.

"That rock, I'll shoot, you run!" Jim screams and punches me lightly on my shoulder. "Go!" He punches Mitt as well.

I half turn, but when Mitt shakes his head, I freeze. Even though I might be safer if I run now, I don't want to do it alone.

"Go!" Jim says, and he slaps Mitt with such power that Mitt almost gets laid out on the ground.

That seems to work, and Mitt leaps past me. I run after him. I hear Jim shooting. I hear the whistles of arrows as they fall. One lands right in front of me. The rock seems further away than I thought. My brain sends the message to my legs to move fast. I stumble over a loose rock. With one swift punch of my hand, I push my upper torso straight and twist my other leg so it catches me. Mitt's behind me. I make it to the rock. It's at a slightly higher position than the previous one.

What am I supposed to do now? Jim is still firing. He has one hand over the rock, firing his weapon. He sees me and nods. I have no clue what it means, because my eyes fixate on the next volley of arrows flying over. Jim has started to run towards us. Mitt makes it to me. I open my mouth to tell Jim to stop.

"Fire!" Mitt yells. He shoots over the rock. I shoot too, aiming for where ever I think a head is. Jim is fast. The old man is a goat. He glides over the rocks and as arrows fall to either side of him, his eyes open wide. But he doesn't slow, and he makes it to our rock in less than a second. And he's off. I don't even notice until Mitt pats me on the shoulder. "Move!"

Men are coming around the rock we were just hiding behind. I shoot at one head that peeks around the corner. The man has long hair that stays still as his head whips back. He falls next to Craig's body. A loud cry goes off from his comrades.

I turn and there's no one there. My heart shudders, my guts straighten themselves out. Luckily, I see a puff of dust and the back of a head as it disappears. I leap and run.

I make it over the rock and hear the whistles of arrows. While running, I fire over my shoulder. Nothing. I'm out. I try to reach for my ammunition, but can't remember which pocket it's in. I reach the top of a cluster of rocks. Mitt and Jim are nowhere to be seen. Did they just leave me? I hear yells behind me. Yells now getting louder.

Taking deep breaths, I think. But I can't think. My mind is a frozen mass; it wants to take in the beautiful rocks and how they seem to form an ocean. Another yell and an arrow goes flying over my head, way over my head. They must be shooting blindly. I pull out some more bullets. Placing each into its chamber, feeling that halt of movement that tells me it's in place.

Another yell. They can't be more than twenty yards out. I need to move. Move.

I'm alone; those bastards left me. That realization hits me, and I feel gravity pull my stomach into my legs, and I can't move. Move you idiot. Try to remember where that truck was kept. Or, barring that, find a place to hide. They'll see you for miles from here.

Running downhill, I see the riverbed with Jim and Mitt running away from me. My heart jolts energy back into my body. I break out into a full sprint. I hear yells, and they sound like they're only a few yards behind me. Did they see me? No time for that.

Follow Jim and Mitt. What the hell are they doing on the riverbed? We'll be picked off easily there. It's the lower ground, and it'll be hard to climb out of. Though a voice tugs me away, my comrades' feet are kicking up powered silt into the air as they run or their lives, and I decide that it's better to be with them than not.

I slip on a rock, as I make it down to the riverbed, and as my ass crunches on the ground an arrow flies past my head. I turn my eyeballs just far enough that I can see several men running towards me. Fifty yards, no more. I fire at them as I lie in on my side. I hit one, and miss the other, but that sends them all scrambling backwards. Except I can hear more yells. It's as if they're all over these hills. I leap back up and jump down to the riverbed. I brace myself with my other arm and stare at the cracked silt. It's smooth. Why am I thinking about this? Run!

Jim and Mitt's heels disappear around the bend. I take off. Willing my legs to move faster, I slash my arms through the air. I'm light; my toes barely touch the ground. Now I'm almost floating. I hear yelling, but it sounds like it's far away. Whistles, but I see no arrows. I'm at the bend. There's a long curve in the riverbed. No sight of Jim or Mitt. I see their footprints. My lungs are now burning. I should have eaten more.

My legs are slowing down. Don't I command. They pick up, but now send shrieks of fire to slow me down. No.

I run out of the curve almost losing my footing. I see Jim and Mitt, they're not so far ahead. My mind's clear. There's danger behind, but I can't look because that'll slow me down. We're getting to where the riverbed leads into a dried up pond. There's something about it that my mind is trying to warn me about.

I catch up to Jim and Mitt just as we land in the pond. Walls of rock rise up before us. I don't turn and brush past them and use my momentum to get halfway up the rock. I grab a hold of an opening between two boulders and pull myself up all the way. Jim is behind me scrambling. Mitt is trying to climb, but can't seem to understand how to hold on to a boulder while finding a way to climb up. In one hand he holds a gun for dear life. He slips. I have half a mind to leave Mitt there, after all what did he do for me?

One glance at the horde of men with arrows, spear and faces that seem destined to eat other men, and I know I can't leave Mitt there. Jim reaches his hand out to me. I pull him up.

The yelling grows louder. The men are no more than a hundred yards away on the riverbed. One of them sees me and his eyes narrow and he bares his teeth. He holds up something: it's Craig's head. Fear mixes in with anger. My ear whines as a rifle fires.

"Come on Mitt, climb!" Jim says as he aims for the men and shoots them. A couple men fall, tumbling and coming to a fantastic stop as the silt around them turns dark red. The other men hide behind rocks and dart forward carefully.

"I can't!" Mitt yells. There's the knowledge of death on his face. He who so wanted to stay by Craig's side until the end.

I swoop down, holding a crack and reach down. "Come on Mitt. Run and try to catch my hand," I say.

Mitt steps back, but a yell frightens him. He raises his rifle and fires. I see the whiplash of a head flying one way while its body flies another.

"Mitt. Put that thing away or else you're going to die there. Run. Jump. Grab my goddamn hand," I say.

Mitt nods, slings his rifle on his shoulder, and takes a few steps back. Arrows fly through the sky. They land harmlessly off the rocks several yards from us. Mitt runs and reaches up. He misses and falls back on his ass. More arrows. This time I clench my teeth as a few come within several feet of me.

"Mitt!" I yell.

Jim yells too and fires a few more shots.

"Let's go!" Jim yells. Mitt takes his rifle into his hands and plays with it. What's he doing?

He grabs the rifle by its barrel and takes another run, with the rifle pointing butt-first at me. Another volley of arrows fly at us. Jim is reloading his rifle; I can hear him swearing. Mitt's rifle butt smacks my fingers, smashes them against the rock and bounces back.

The streak of pain from what seems to be my crushed fingers flashes through my body. The arrows are frozen mid-flight. I push the pain out of mind and snap at the rifle butt, holding it right where the shoulder strap is attached. I grasp the butt firmly and pull with all my might. The butt slips, but I clench even harder. Swift arrowheads are all I see, and I close my eyes. I pull-swing the rifle up and to me. The sound of a rifle firing again, and arrowheads landing around me, fill me with dread. I open my eyes and see Mitt sweating, with clammy skin, looking at me and he gives a half-smile. He's breathing funny.

"Hold on," I say and turn my back to him. He clasps his hands around my shoulders, and I climb up. When I get to the top, Jim is reloading another magazine.

"Let's get the hell outta here!" Jim yells. He pulls out a grenade and throws it into the pond bottom, just as some of our pursuers run into it. All three of us hit the ground and the explosion shakes the ground and my head.

We take off. This time we're on a ridge and though we're going fast as we can, the boulders that stand in our way slow us down. Mitt slows down, clutching his left leg and below his right arm. I yell, and he comes after us.

When I look around, I see heads ducking behind rocks. Not just directly behind us on our trail, but to our flanks as well. I shudder when I think that we might well be surrounded. My muscles are tired, and I feel like my ribcage can't take anymore expanding and contracting. Craig's dangling head, and that man's eyes as he was being burned, runs through my head and I pick up my pace.

Mitt falls behind again, and I drop back to grab him. He's limping. I notice that one of the arrows sliced him pretty deep into his thigh. I look at his ribcage and notice bone jutting out. He must have been hit there too. I throw one of his arms over my shoulders and run with him. He gets heavier and heavier as we keep running.

"The truck!" Jim yells, his voice on a wire now.

I think about the men surrounding us. Surely they must have out flanked us by now, especially with Mitt slowing us down. "Be careful!" I yell. Jim doesn't seem to hear me, so I reach out and grab his shoulder. "They know where it is," I say.

We're down near where the hills meet the flat plains, and the truck is off to the right. The camouflage netting is still on, but something's not right.

"What do you mean?" Jim says, spit flying out of his mouth. "We have to get out of here, and now."

I nod and point my pistol at the rocks near the truck.

Jim slaps down my gun. "What the hell are you doing?"

"They already know," I say. Two heads move next to a boulder near the truck.

Jim whips his head back in time to see them. "Goddamit."

"We need to get out of range," I say. "On the plains their arrows are worthless once we get out of range."

"The truck. If they learn how to start it, we're dead anyways."

I'm not certain where Jim kept the keys. They could be in the truck for all I know. I take a grenade and throw it towards the truck. I hear yelling from behind us. Mitt steps away from me, and holding his side, he lobs a grenade behind us. We duck and two explosions go off one after the other. Screams sound off after the second one. I jump up and see that the truck has part of its netting blown off, but is otherwise untouched. A crater hole lies beside it.

"How many grenades?" I ask.

"I have three," Jim says.

"One," Mitt says.

I grab Mitt's grenade, and I throw it again at the truck. We duck behind a rock and see a slew of arrows flying through the sky. It's blind shooting, but it shows that they still have plenty more ammunition than we do. Another explosion rips the air. I hear metal landing on the rocks.

I turn to see the truck's on fire. The camouflage netting is off and two charred bodies lie on the front seats. Next to the car, a man curls up, flames dancing off his charred body. He's a tight ball now and stops moving. A sigh of relief goes up from Jim's lips. Mitt's whiter than a ghost, and when I touch his skin it's cold. He's shivering.

I look through my pockets and realize that I don't have many bullets.

"I'm almost out," I say.

Mitt fires off a round at a rock, and I take his arm. We start running, past a few boulders and into the open plains. Jim spins and takes a knee shooting a few rounds. "Run," he says.

I run with Mitt. When the shooting stops hurting my ears, I turn and start shooting. "Run," I yell. Jim runs at us.

Mitt places his rifle stock on my shoulder and starts firing. My ears are mosquitoes soon and it stops bothering me. My pistol isn't much use; we're at least a hundred yards away. I'm sure we're safe.

A few of the men make dashes forward, but Mitt picks one of them out and the rest of them hide behind the last boulders dripping forth from the hills.

Jim rushes by us. His footsteps retreat behind me. The next volley of arrows whistles through the air. I watch, first chuckling to myself since I'm sure that the arrows won't make it to us, then my heart freezes as the arrows slice through air and come right at us. It's too late to run. I drop and shield myself with my arms. I'm sure I'm dead.

I close my eyes. I hear Mitt moving, I assume he's falling. The arrows land with sharp slaps off the earth. One of the arrows, however, hits something soft. I hear a groan. I look up, surprised that my flesh hasn't been penetrated. Mitt's standing in front of me, blocking the arrows.

"Run!" Jim yells.

Jim looks to be a hundred yards further away from us. I cuss, he could have stopped sooner and…

I grab Mitt, but he's stiff. There are two arrows jutting out from his stomach and shoulder. His eyes are wide open, and he's trying to say something. I grab him, throw him over my shoulder and run as fast as I can. Another volley of arrows whistles through the air. By the time they land I'm too far-gone. I stop next to Jim and drop Mitt to the ground. He doesn't say anything.

Jim looks him over and taps his face. "Mitt? Buddy?"

Mitt slowly opens his eyes. "Don't leave me here with them, Jim. Don't," he whispers. His face's dead white. I grab a bottle of water from his backpack. Jim shakes his head.

"He's dead." He closes his eyes. "Dammit. Sorry Mitt. Sorry," he says.

I turn to the hills, I see a few men breaking from the boulders. There will be no time to rest. I grab Mitt's rifle and aim. Slowly, I pull the trigger. One of the men falls. The others hit the ground. The rest run back to the boulders. The truck is still burning.

"Were there any weapons on that truck?" I ask.

"No," Jim says. "But plenty of fuel and ammo."

"We can't wait here," I say.

Jim doesn't answer. He props a grenade underneath Mitt's body, the pin off, the spoon still on.

"Let's go," he says. I take Mitt's bag, and we take off in a trot.

My legs are tired and I want to sleep so badly.

After a few minutes, Jim turns and takes a knee. The hills stand small, but the truck still burns. A series of shots go off, tracers shoot from the truck. I hear yells and screams, and I laugh.

There are men spread across the plains. They have all dropped now that Jim has turned. He cusses and gets up. "When it gets dark we're screwed. Then our gun advantage is no good."

What can I say? I'm not even scared.

We trot again. This time I run backwards. I see a few of them stand up. I stop and I shoot. They all drop. I miss.

"Don't waste anything more," Jim says. "And save one for yourself."

We trot on. The sun is fast approaching the horizon. I turn a few more times, but don't see any more men. We hear an explosion.

"Thanks Mitt," Jim says. "You killed one more."

We stop near a half-buried old axle of a car. It's hardly rusted. We stop and eat. "Wonder how old the car was," I say, staring at this relic of manufacturing.

Jim shrugs. "Why does it matter?"

It doesn't matter, but what's wrong with knowing? Maybe there was a highway here way back when.

"I don't see anyone," I say as we get up. I wonder how much food we have left, and how long it will take to get back.

"Keep moving," he says.

"What if they follow the tire tracks home?" I ask.

"We went through some rock, to get here, so that should throw them off."

"Not if they're persistent."

We start trotting again.

"Can you smell them?" Jim asks.

I stop and sniff. Nothing. "There's no wind."

He keeps on trotting. I catch up. My legs don't hurt anymore; in fact they feel weightless. "How long?" I ask.

"I don't remember," he says.

"Do we know the right direction?"

He points to the side. I see our tire tracks. "We'll be easy to follow," I say.

Jim doesn't answer.

The sun sparks up half the sky as it falls down. I half pray that it stays above the horizon for as long as possible. Deep down I know that's foolish, but I want some sort of help from a higher power. God if you can hear me, help me.

I ask a few more questions. Jim doesn't answer. He seems to be in a trance.

"They were good men," I say.

"What the hell would you know about that?" he snaps without looking my way.

My empathy evaporates, and I imagine myself throwing the old man to the ground and punching through his face. That thought lingers, and I try to wash it out of my head. I need to be nicer. I cuss myself out for leaving Genevine. But where would that have left these men? I look at Jim's form trudging next to me. Wasn't it his fault that we assumed we were safe in the hills? But who sent us out here to bleed those men with a hair-brained scheme?

We stop running. Jim is too tired. I turn and squint. Dusk has fallen and it's hard to see movement on the horizon. The top of the mountain we climbed is gone. I sniff the air. Still nothing. When the sky has completely leaked out all daylight, I can barely see Jim. There's no moon and a few clouds cover the otherwise brilliant stars. Another satellite flies over us.

We stop and sit down.

"You see that?" I say, pointing to the hurried light above us.

Jim sits down and starts to eat. "I see it," he says after a long pause. He pulls out food. "Better eat as much as you can. And don't talk. They'll hear us."

I lean in to whisper. "If they're following us." Should I let him know that this was partially his fault? That'll cut him down to size. I eat. All of Mitt's food. We really didn't pack much.

We do guard shifts. Luckily, Jim has an old watch to help keep track. I take the first one. Not certain what I'm supposed to do; I decide to stand up and see more. A chilly wind picks up and I sit back down. It's winter, or at least I think it is, and yet it hasn't been as cold as I thought it'd be.

The outline of the hills and flat plains is clearer now. Below that I can't see much. If they're still following us they could easily surround us. Then what? Save a bullet for ourselves, I suppose.

Genevine's smell, touch, floats into my brain. I miss her. Why would these men be following us when they could easily turn back home and be with their women?

And I remember Craig's dangling head. I imagine they're doing the same with Mitt's remains. What were we trying to accomplish coming out here? Remember the man being burned alive. What if you had found these people instead? You'd have been eaten alive. Not me, I argue with myself. This voice, probably the same one that helped to push Jenny off the cliff, speaks up. You don't know what you're thinking. John sent you here, and it's John's fault.

My mind's in that torture room with MacGee again. He's looking at me, asking me to save him. And I can't. I'm in the shack with Jenny, the first time I saw her. Then that night when I came back from

Portland with the knowledge that I would never see my wife again, knowing that I had only survived because of violence. And John reaching out his hand to me so that I could kiss it. *He* was the reason MacGee was dead.

The smell of men fills my nostrils and I snap up, awake. Jim is lying next to me asleep and the sun is already above the hills. I look around but don't see anything. The wind picks up, and I smell them as clear as day. Did I fall asleep before I woke up Jim?

I punch him and he grumbles. I place my finger on his lips. "They're here," I say. His eyes widen, and he raises his rifle.

"Better eat first," he says. "We'll need our energy if this is going to be the last stand."

Eating, I keep an eye on the horizon. The smell only appears when the wind picks up, blowing from the place we're running from. I finish half of what's left.

"Eat more," Jim says. "This might be the last one you get."

A drop in the pit of my stomach. I've been through worse, I tell myself. I count out my remaining bullets. Twenty. Mitt's add up to no more than fifteen. My guts extend through my body. The ground gives way. Keep it together. If this is it, then give them hell. I squeeze the weakness out of my body with everything I have.

When we're done eating, we start moving. I keep an eye out. I smell, but I can't see. I start jogging, but Jim grunts in response. "You tired?" I ask.

"Of course."

He's still angry with me? The wind picks up, and I smell the men again. They must be closing in. I look over at Jim. We might as well talk. I think of Craig's dangling head. That's not the best topic in the world. My mind crawls, then suddenly snaps at something.

"The insects," I say, hitting Jim.

He furrows his forehead and regards me with a malice I've not seen since the days I crawled out of that cave.

"None of the bodies were eaten by insects."

"So?" Jim asks, his neck twisting as he looks about.

"Maybe they're gone for ever."

"No food," Jim says.

"Or…" I try to think of something better, but that seems like the only reasonable answer. Don't think about that, think about surviving. "Stop."

"We have to keep moving," Jim says.

"Grasp your hands together. I'm going to climb up you and see if I can see them better.

I get up on his interlaced hands and crane my neck trying to see anything. Nothing. Our footsteps, the car tires. Nothing else. I take another sniff. Something like feces this time. That can't be the men. What was I smelling before? "I don't see them."

"Do you smell them?"

"I smell something. I'm not sure if it's them. It's…" I decide not to say anything else. I squint to see if there's any movement at all. It's not like there are trees to hide behind. All the rocks out here on the plain are no larger than my head. They couldn't possibly be hiding.

"You planning on staying up there all day?" Jim says.

I look down on his head. He really is on edge. "Maybe."

He cusses under his breath.

"Hold on," I say, half smiling to myself.

"Do you see them or don't you," he says, the strain in his voice is now obvious.

"I'm trying. Almost…"

He's breathing hard now.

"What're you looking at?" he asks, breathing harder and harder.

"You."

He undoes his hands and lets me fall to the ground. I expected it, but I fall on a stone. Nevertheless, I yelp and laugh.

He shakes his head. "You gonna to laugh when we're about to die?"

"And so what?" I say. "If we're going to die anyways?"

"And you'll make sure they know where we're at," he says.

My childish glee disappears and I stand up, dusting myself off and face off with him. "What the hell, Jim? You have a problem with me?"

"Yeah, I do," he says. "It was your grand plan to take them down. How did that work out for you?" He's an inch away from my face, and spittle flies out and lands on my cheek. His breath smells like the wrong end of a dog.

I try to remember how exactly the plan folded out. I'm not sure about the details, but... "You're the military guy, aren't you? And you said that you came up with the plan first."

"I was only humoring you."

"And don't give me shit about this being my fault," I say. "You were the brilliant one who said they were scared of those rocks. You were the one who got us here." I stab my finger at his chest. I feel some vindication when his face softens, though it hardens right back up.

"Fuck you," he says. "You and your friend John are the ones who want these fights. It's because of ya'll we're in this mess."

"You're blaming John for this?" I ask.

"Of course I am. You think I want to be out here starting fights for no reason?" he says, his voice cracking at the edges. "Those two kids were like my sons. And they're gone. Probably being eaten." He turns away, his eyes glistening.

My heart expands. "Sorry, Jim," I say. He does remind me of MacGee, and the parts that aren't like MacGee are like me. I grasp his shoulder. "Sorry." The smells of the men are growing stronger. I keep an eye on the horizon behind us.

Jim throws off my hand with a heave of his shoulder. "What the hell do you care? You're with John, aren't you?" His voice is back to being solid and angry.

"I—"

"You're just like him. You're a leader, right? A cold bastard making those decisions. Right? We listen to what you say. So then take responsibility."

He's still not facing me.

"But you won't. Didn't even lift a finger for your friend, did you? All you cared about was getting some power," he says.

That slaps the air out of my lungs. I don't know whether to be angry or hurt.

"Just like every person who's a leader. Like the men who caused this whole mess. I thought we could start something new, but it's always the same. Always will be. And now even more people will die," Jim says.

I don't say anything. I can't say anything.

The wind whips around my feet, sand tunneling its way around it, making a quiet crashing-crystals sound.

"Can you smell them?" Jim asks after a long pause.

I sniff the air. I looking at the horizon for movement, but in actuality I'm thinking about that torture room where I last talked to MacGee. I killed him.

"They're getting closer," I say. The smell of feces is replaced by that of the men. Whatever it is—damp body parts and unwashed clothes?—it's getting stronger. Now I don't need the wind to smell them.

We take off. I try to focus on the ground in front of me. Dodge this stone, or this rivet, and jump over that mound of dirt. It helps take the sting off Jim's words.

Anger bubbles up. At me, Jim, the world. I spin with the rifle and aim at the horizon. One bobbing head's too slow to react, as the others hit the dirt. I hold my breath and fire.

A hail Mary shot, really, but the snap of the head, the thump sound of the bullet impacting, are all distinct and fill me with glee. There's a half wail or sound of surprise, and the man falls to his knees.

"Good shot," Jim says.

Anger still powering me, I train my rifle on a hump on the ground as it moves. It's a man crawling. Any shot will do damage, I think. I fire and see a mist of pink in the air. A scream cuts through the air, and fills my heart with something other than self-loathing. I smile. They're too brave, within a couple hundred meters. I shoot at another lump that's trying to push itself into the ground as far as possible. Dirt is kicked up. But the message is sent; the man gets up and runs in a zig-zag fashion away from us. A few others do the same. Off and on. They're too smart and disciplined to take off running at the same time. Some send arrows our way, but they fall harmlessly in front of us. I aim at a few more and miss. Now there's another feeling inside me. It heats my head, churns my body. I'm not sure what it is.

"Enough," Jim says.

We turn and run. I keep an eye on our tail ends, but it's hard to see if they've stopped following us, or have just fallen further behind.

After what seems to be an eternity we resort to walking. The sun is already on its way down. We're out of water and running will only make things worse. We eat the last of our food.

The men aren't emitting any smell. The wind's also dead, though, so I can't be sure. The sun falls. It gets cooler. That means we'll need less water, but it also means that we won't be able to see the men. A few jagged orange hill-rocks are in front of us. Jim says those are the ones where we can lose the men. I doubt that. It means we can be ambushed there too.

"This is foolish. How many days are we from our compound?"

Jim shrugs.

"Don't you have a map?"

He taps his head.

I do the calculation. We were traveling around forty miles an hour. Half a day. "We could be more than a hundred miles from home. You realize that, right?"

"What can we do about it?"

"We don't have water. We need water. It's going to take at least a few days, if not a couple weeks, to get back home. If we walk they'll just tire us out. Then what?"

The sun's an orange ball in the sky. "They haven't traveled this far without food and water. They must have lots of it."

"And do you expect them to just give it over?"

"We attack them."

"They'll see us. We may get a couple, but they'll overpower us eventually."

"Not at night they won't."

"What?" Jim asks.

"I said: not at night they won't see us."

"You want to attack them at night?"

"Why not. It's obvious they're sleeping at night, right?"

"And you're going to take their food? You understand it'll be bits and pieces of Mitt and Craig, right?"

That idea stops my planning for a second. A growl in my stomach sets the planning back in motion. I have to eat. "We need the water at least. And besides they might have more than meat."

"You won't be able to sneak up on them," Jim says.

"Why not? They won't be able to see us."

"Because if they have half a brain they spread out in the day so it's hard to shoot many of them at once, and at night they'll group up together with some of them standing guard."

He has a perfect military mind, this Jim.

"But they still can't see anything. And I'm going to assume they can't smell us either, otherwise they would've killed us back in the hills."

Jim relaxes. "Then we'd better pray for some clouds."

He's right about that, the sky isn't clear, but there are cracks. We don't need a flash of moonlight highlighting our position. We keep walking. The hills before us grow. We might be but a few hours away from them. The earth glooms.

That feeling, from when I shot the men, from the eruption of memories, lingers in my stomach.

"You really think we'll be safe in those hills?" I ask.

"It might help to hide."

"I wonder how far they're willing to follow us."

"We entered their place, killed their men. If I were them, I'd come pretty far."

That doesn't help.

The sun splashes into the horizon's pool and orange red ripples off. Purple invades, and I take one more look behind us. No movement, and I can't smell them. But I see our footprints, and the tire tracks off to the side. They can take their time following us.

We walk, and we start to stumble over stones and divots. The sky is dark with clouds.

"You sure about this?" Jim asks.

"You thirsty?"

"Yup."

Jim's question digs into my psyche. We might not be able to do this. They might be expecting this and set up a trap for us. And that thought cascades into fear. And unlike before, perhaps because I have so much time to think about it, it sucks the energy out of me, and that only makes me feel that this is truly my last moment on earth. Funny that I'd come so far, survived so many people, and then this. The flash of being chosen was a strong hope to hold on to, that and it's implied divinity. But now I'm feeling more like a lucky fool. And the more I feel like this, the more I think about the things I did. Jenny. Her innocence robbed by me; her life destroyed because of me. And MacGee. A friend I killed. To save myself or gain power?

"I'm not like John," I say. At the same time I say this my mind is trying to jettison every reason I came up with to help, or follow John. Even the moment I kissed his hand. Kneeled before him. Even the pledge I made. Even the God I thought I was fighting for.

"I didn't mean it," Jim says.

"You did. And it makes sense. I'm not like him, though."

"I know."

He doesn't. "I've done some bad things, Jim. You're right; I killed MacGee. I shot him, and he was my friend."

Jim lets out some air, as if he's trying to lighten his load. "I didn't mean it like that. I know he tried to kill John."

I turn to face him. It's quiet and there's no wind. For a moment all I smell is clean air. Then foul Jim's body odor. "When I was in that room with him, seeing him clutching on to life, I wanted to help him. I thought that maybe I could help him escape. When I realized that was impossible, I shot him. Out of mercy. But he wanted to be saved."

As I speak my mind drips acid into my body. The pain pushes a shudder through me.

I can barely make out Jim's face. It's etched charcoal on black.

My heart beats in my chest, broken and tired. "I'm not like John. Not in some ways." But I think: *am* I really that different from John? We both saw ways to survive, gain power, and we did.

"You're not," he says.

I feel more the fool for expecting some revelation from Jim, or some words that will lift all of my sins. Is there ever such a thing? Not from a man. The sky perhaps? I look up and it's dark; the clouds have covered the star and moonlight very well. So there will be no light to disinfect me.

"I killed many people before that," I say.

"We all did. It was tough. We had to survive," Jim says.

"Not all of it was to survive," I say. I remember the look in Bill's eyes when he recognized me. I remember "please don't" and Jenny's soft smooth skin squirming underneath me. My body, foolish body, is tantalized. My brain secretes more acid and the desire is gone. "I killed men as they begged."

"All men beg. Doesn't mean you could have survived otherwise," Jim says.

Does he even understand what I'm trying to say? The wind picks up and my brain, soaked in treacherous memories, picks up the scent of the men. They're close. I brush that off. Survival is nothing without a sense of cleanliness.

"I took an innocent girl and drive her to her death," I say.

The silence this time is different. I can feel my words punch through Jim's stolid facade.

"I did..." I repeat.

"It's hard..." Jim says.

I don't feel any better.

"Why are you saying all this?" Jim asks.

"No reason," I say. That's a lie; there's always a reason. The wind cuts between us, cold and sharp. "We should get this over with."

I pull out my handgun and grip it in one hand. In the other I have Mitt's rifle. Jim is double fisting as well.

We turn and walk perpendicular to our tracks. It's Jim's idea. I push all the bad images and memories out of my mind. But they release a foul anger that seeps into my movements. Now I hope that maybe when I bleed I'll be able to cleanse myself. And I walk towards the men, sniffing, hoping to run into them. Blood is all I want.

After a few minutes we lurch towards where the men should be. The night is still. We're taking slow high steps so that we land flat-footed. It keeps us quiet and from tripping over obstacles. I can see the outline of hills and flat plains level with my eye. What's in directly in front of me, however, only appears as shadows and darker shadows. And the border between the two is hard to make out.

When the wind picks up several minutes later, I freeze and grab Jim's sleeve. We can't talk, not even a whisper, but they're here. Somewhere.

I try to listen to see if one of them is snoring. Nothing, just the wind flipping over grains of sand, and blood tightening my muscles. Jim mentioned once that I should look above an object at night if I wanted to see it. I stare off at the horizon. An outline near me appears. I look over and it's gone. I look above it and it fades in. I gulp in deep breaths.

Where are the rest of them?

Jim's fingers dig into my right hand, and I glance at where he guides my hand. Above it. A huddle of black. I'm regretting having ever come up with this thought. Don't think about what they did to that man, or Craig's dangling head. Think about cleansing yourself. If you die, do it for Jenny and MacGee. Join them.

Energized, I take a step towards the man who's huddling alone. He must be a guard. A few more steps and I see that it's two men. I see our tracks. I gag at the aroma of freshly grilled meat.

Jim is next to me. He points at one. I move over to the other side, shouldering my rifle, stuffing my handgun, and pulling out a knife. It has to be quiet. I'm not certain how to do this. The throat, right? Jim is nodding at me. Does that mean now? I can't hear anything but my own breathing. Surely this is a foolish idea? Maybe we should back out now and try to run. Maybe if we run all night we'll get away. Jim raises his hand. He's going for it.

Cleanse yourself, you coward.

I move in with two hands, one meant to stifle his mouth if he screams. But the throat, I have to cut through the throat. All the way through. In my periphery Jim is moving towards his man. I come close, move my head closer, because I can't really tell where his throat is, only where his head is and where his torso is. For the briefest moment I reconsider my actions, but the knife is moving. It's too late. I'm off balance and I have to fall on him. It's me or him now.

My free hand touches his face. His lips, moist, wet, and his face starts to spasm. My knife strikes. The lips are here so I must slice there. My knife hits what has to be his neck as he jerks. It's the jerk of a man still asleep. I clasp my hand over his mouth. And with the knife I slice and thrust as furiously as I can. It slides into something, the man jerks and his hands flail. I hold his mouth tight, though a muffled cry leaks out. In this quiet night it explodes in the air.

No time. The man is kicking. I jerk the knife again. Resistance, but it's giving way with the certainty that only flesh could. I'm in. I'm sure, because the man's cries are no longer passing his lips, they're gurgling up his throat. I slice, back and forth, trying to get through it all. Warm liquid engulfs my hand. He flails around, and I hold tight. Then the stillness. I stop. I'm sweating.

The world is my heart and exhalations. Jim is by my side. He guides me to lie down. The black form he was supposed to take care of is still. I lie on my belly, beside the corpse. I almost feel attached to the man. My belly grows wet from his warm leakage.

The group of black shadows to our front stirs. I see the outline of a man sitting up. He's looking around. After a few seconds he falls back down. We wait. I almost fall asleep. My wet clothes turn cold and keep me awake.

Jim gets up first. Each man has a small knapsack. We grab it. He shows me his grenades, and he places one under the man he killed. Following Jim's lead, I crouch and take small steps. We're duck walking. Makes sense. Above a certain height everything is outlined by the sky, as dark as it may be. I feel my heart in my throat. I taste blood.

When we get to the group of men, we're sliding with our bellies on the ground. My heart throbs like it's ready to rebel. I can see the lumps; there are scores of them. Jim reaches over and grabs a hold of a bag. An inch every half-minute, he pulls it to his chest. He nods at me, and I slide and do the same. Every move I make, I hold my breath trying to see how loud it truly is. When sand that's stuck to my sleeves falls to the ground, I freeze. When my clothes seemingly crackle in the night, I hold my breath and listen. Clothes have never been so loud. I calm myself with the thought that I will take as many of them as possible.

Pulling a bag towards me, the nearest man stirs. I freeze. He mumbles something. Don't wake up.

A few seconds later, deep breaths rumble from his chest. With the bag in hand I grab a hold of another. Jim taps me, with a shake of his head. He's right; with a bag in each hand I'll find it hard to move. We make our way back, crawling backwards on our bellies, keeping an eye on the men. We back up past the two dead men.

Jim shows me another grenade. He leans into my ear and whispers: "We'll throw it when we get a little further out."

I just want to leave. Why risk missing and having them come after us?

We walk for a few minutes.

"This too far?" Jim asks.

"No." I take the grenade from him.

"Pull the pin then throw. One motion," he says. "Don't hesitate. The spoon—"

"I've already done this, remember?" I say, not wanting to be talked to like a child. I hold the grenade in my hand and pull the pin. I throw it as hard as I can, stumbling forward after I do. Jim hits the ground; I do too. Waiting those few seconds to hear a slight thud, to hope that the grenade at least fell within striking distance of the men, clears my mind. And still that feeling in my guts lingers. Will I ever be able to cleanse myself?

I wait. Is the grenade a dud? Will the men wake up and follow us?

The explosion rips the air, shakes my brain and fills my chest with solid-state air. The sand around me jumps. When the screams fill the air, I breathe them in. It's the sound of the men who killed Craig and Mitt dying. And somehow I feel a little cleaner.

Jim pats me on the back and we stand up. It's impossible to see, of course. But I hear the cries of men calling to each other.

"Mark! Where are you?" one voice shrieks above the chorus of groans.

I didn't envision any of them having such names. I try not to dwell on it. The wind picks up, and I smell the clear blood, the gaseous chemicals from the grenade, and flesh. Their flesh.

"Mark! Don't!" More screams punctuate the air.

Jim taps me. "Let's get going, in case they decide to come after us once and for all. It won't be hard to track us, and at best that grenade's radius only killed a few of them."

We turn and run. Not that fast though, my legs don't have the energy, but with enough speed that we're soon out of smell range and the groans and cries fade into an indiscernible hum. We head for the hills and after an hour we reach them.

Jim finds a flat-topped boulder to lie on top of. It's at least fifty feet above the plains. We each go through our bags. There are rations, thank God. I eat one of my bags as fast as I can. It tastes like powder, but my stomach sucks it in, and I can feel my muscles sigh.

Torches light up on the plains. They're far away, enough that their actions are silent ones from another planet. More than a mile, we won't be able to pick them with a rifle from here. I can see a pile of bodies. Are they going to eat them?

"I wonder if they eat their own?" I ask.

"Does it matter?" Jim asks.

I fall asleep.

An explosion wakes me up, though now it's just a distant echo. Jim stirs from his sleep. I see the torches, one landing from its flight. More congregate. It's hard to see what they're doing. They're pointing, and some seem to be fighting. That's hopeful, but what gets me down is that there are still plenty of them to keep on running after us. But they don't know that we have any more grenades, do they? Surely it's madness on their part to come after us.

Jim mutters something, and rubs his head with his hand. He's asleep, but his face cracks into a smile. He was right about me. I am like John. Maybe I'm even like those men chasing us. Does it even matter what I'm like? It was John's fault that we came on this expedition. And it's his fault that MacGee is dead. That knot in my stomach, that dreaded feeling that I thought I would never get rid of, lightens its grip on me.

John, his Kingdom of Heaven, all that was a charade. I'm sure of it. As the torches go dark and the plain is reduced to a single dark unknown, I close my eyes and fall asleep.

The next day I walk up to see a slip of the sun on the horizon. Jim is sitting next to me eating.

"You think about your wife often?" he asks.

His voice has none of the sharpness from yesterday. "Yes," I say. I don't think about Carol as much as I should. In fact, after losing Jenny, someone I didn't know for that long, I couldn't really think about Carol at all. Any thoughts about her, the memories, the passion, the touches and the moans, were superseded by those moments with Jenny. It was as if the neural pathways for Carol are, or were, too weak. I hate myself for this.

"I think about mine all the time," Jim says. "Wonder why I had her go into the city to buy a few things. We weren't fighting or nothing. And yet I didn't want to deal with her for a few days so I told her to go on and leave me be." He shakes his head. "I was thinking that shopping with her would be annoying. I was also thinking of spending some time with one of the younger girls at the camp." He looks down at his food. The wrinkles on his face seem deeper than yesterday.

"You can't blame yourself," I say, not really knowing what to say, but that's the only thing that comes to mind. And then I think that it's a little too blasé, and that maybe I only said it because I heard it somewhere in a movie.

"How can I not?"

"I don't know, but you have to. Otherwise what's the use of going on?"

Jim chews on his food, the crunches muffled by his flesh.

"Even I have a reason to blame myself. I left my wife to do something she never liked. If I'd listened to her maybe I would have been with her. Saved her."

"Maybe not."

"That wouldn't have been the worst thing, would it?"

Feeling something close to a revelation, I look away, trying to make out if the shadows in the distance are the men in pursuit.

"Before the fall," Jim says. "We used to take trips to California. Yosemite Park. Beautiful place. We would pay for a campsite near the west end and spend a week just hiking. Something else... to be amongst the trees, nature." He picks up his rifle. There's something vindictive about the way he's doing it, and I tense up, expecting him to fire it. Whether it's at me or himself, I can't tell.

"We wanted to take our son there one day. But when they came things got too busy. With John... no extraneous travels." Jim spits on the ground. "All I can think about are the times in bed, when the son came, and how she worried about him. I'd hold her hand, wondering why she stressed so much... Now I can see why."

My mind pictures a softer Jim holding his woman's hand. I remember holding Carol's hand during our many walks through our suburban neighborhood, or the many sunsets we'd watch.

"What the hell is this all for?" Jim asks. "What the hell does John want to accomplish sending us out here?"

His tone implies that he includes me with John. "I don't know Jim, I really don't."

"Yes you do," he says, pointing his finger at me, as he trembles. "You know exactly what was going through his mind. Why else would you have come with us?"

"I just wanted to come along," I say, though I feel like a fool for using that as an excuse.

"We didn't have a choice," he says.

He hits me hard with that fact. "Kingdom of Heaven," I say.

"What?"

"We were doing it for His Kingdom."

"Whose? John's?"

"No, God's. We wanted to expand it. That's what he did at the caves," I say. The words leave my mouth and come back through my brain filtered of all prejudice. And what had I thought at the caves, of Thomas? MacGee thought the same thing, except he was willing to risk his life.

"You really believe that?" Jim says.

"I don't know. It was comforting."

"Killing people is comforting?"

"You did the same," I say. "Weren't you the tactics master?"

"What else could I do? Get us all killed? John doesn't..."

"You were only following orders, right?" I say. I'm not happy about putting him on the spot, because I somewhat agree with him. But sharing the blame with him helps. "And besides, look at these men and what they did. They were cannibals," I say, remembering that man who burned.

"And if we hadn't come out here, they wouldn't have bothered us." Jim kicks a few rocks with his feet, and stares out at the rising sun. "The only Kingdom worth fighting for is one of peace. I mean, look at this," he says and points at the wasteland before us. "This was something until we fought it into nothing. And you're telling me that doing more of the same is going to create a better world?"

"No... We can change."

"How? It's all the same in the end, and this is what John wants, isn't it?"

"And if you help me, we can stop him," I say.

He weighs these words, rocking his head back and forth. "Impossible. John has a grip on the council. And each council member—"

"Aren't they scared of him? Isn't that what you said?"

"They are. But they also believe that he talks to God," Jim replies.

"Does he?" I ask.

Jim turns to eye me, a snarl on his face. "Christ," he says.

The sun now lights our part of the earth, and I stand up next to Jim to see if the men have moved. I see nothing.

"Too far to see them unless they move," Jim says.

"You think they left at night?"

"They could've."

I feel comfortable with Jim by my side, knowing that he hates John. Staring at the nothingness of the land, I try to remember a time before the fall when I saw such a scene. The closest thing was the desert in New Mexico. Though even then there was sign of life, a plane overhead, a highway whining in the distance. What I see now reminds me more of pictures of Mars. Imagine that: the world visited by aliens in the future who will look at our planet and try to find signs of us. As a child, stories of civilization lost on Mars intrigued me for I always saw Mars as that: a cautionary tale for us. I grew up, I'd thought.

"You going after John?" Jim asks.

It's hard to tell if he's in awe or just curious.

"We agree that a certain lifestyle isn't in accordance with what we want," I say. Why am I trying to be effuse? If Jim is on my side I will need him.

"Agreed," he says. "We have to change the course."

I feel vindicated, now that he seems to be on board. A plan, I need a plan. How *are* coups done? "We can't vote him out, can we?"

"No votes," Jim replies.

My heart rate picks up, my mind tightens. I try to think of the third world countries where this happened. They used the military, didn't they? But there was always something else. What was it?

"So…" I say. "Do the other soldiers listen to you?"

Jim nods.

I want more from him, not some halfhearted gesture. I twist to face him. I place my hand on his shoulder. I can't force anything here; he has to do this on his own. "Are you with me?"

"I am."

That's all I need. "And the other soldiers will be with you?"

"We might have to explain it some other way," he says.

"Do they enjoy the fighting?"

"When they're winning, sure."

"But not if they're dying?"

"That's right," Jim answers and sniffs.

I'm sure Jim can explain that much to them. "And the council members?"

"That will be tough. They represent heads of most the families."

What I care about are the men who know violence.

"I think we should get a move on," I say. There's no sign of our pursuers.

"It's not going to be easy," Jim says.

"To get away?" I ask.

"No, to stop John. He's a tough man, and a smart bastard too."

"Those council members," I say, remembering that even Jim was scared of John because of how John dealt with those council members.

"One thought he could do it behind John's back, to usurp him, but it wasn't to be."

"Someone ratted him out?" I ask, wondering if one of the soldiers will do the same.

"No, John saw it on his face. Dragged him out and finished him off."

I think of MacGee's screams. John has outwitted everyone so far.

I breathe in condensed sand and feel the weak sunrays tickle my skin. I'm tired and can't wait to be home. Genevine's smell as she rubbed my stomach reaches out from the depths of my mind and caresses me. I want to be with her, to feel her warmth on my chest. Do I really want to start a coup?

"We can't do it at once," Jim says, as if sensing my thoughts.

"The soldiers?"

"That's right. We'll have to measure them out."

The gap between knowing what I want—to stop John—and being able to achieve that widens. How could I possibly think to trust that many soldiers? That many people? One of them would sooner or later talk to one of the council members, or John.

"Measure them out," I say.

"Slowly."

"Or we could push John towards peace. Tell him that we can take it easy on the fighting."

The wind picks up. We're downwind from the men, and I don't smell anything. "We should get going," I say.

We walk through the hills and rocks for several hours. The clouds above us cover the sun and a wind with a sharp cold rises. Maybe winter will finally come.

We stay as long as we can in the hills, hoping that the hard rocks will throw our pursuers off our track. I'm not entirely comfortable here. Around every corner a potential ambush lurks, and I tense my hands around my pistol just in case. Jim doesn't seem to care, and keeps his head down, watching his step.

Stopping for lunch, we eat the remains of another bag.

"How much farther do you think we have to go?" I ask.

Jim shrugs.

"I think only a couple of days." I don't say anything about Jim's actions, but I don't like it. This is supposed to be my partner in crime? I expect more.

No reply.

The wind shifts and my skin prickles. That sets off my mind. What if we didn't see the men because they'd decided to outflank us? They tried it on the rocks when they ambushed us, so why wouldn't they do it here? I glance around and see nothing. That distinct aroma I smelled a second ago is nowhere amongst these rocks.

"What's wrong? Smell something?" Jim asks.

"No. Something's wrong." If they were hell bent on revenge after we had killed a few of their friends, enough so they'd follow us for that distance, then why wouldn't they be more bent on revenge now?

"You're getting twitchy."

"We didn't see them, did we?"

Jim rolls his eyes.

I hear something. Barely, maybe even so slight a noise that normally I'd attribute it to my mind's imagination. But right here and now, I know there's something out there. It wasn't the wind pushing something.

We're eating in a place that's in the way of an avenue between the rocks. It's the perfect place to be ambushed. To my right there's a crop of rocks that rises a few feet above our heads. To my left there's a high face of cracked boulders that climbs out of sight.

"Climb," I whisper, adjusting my weapons and backpack.

"What for?" he says in a hushed voice.

"Do it now," I whisper and start climbing.

"They're not going to be here," he says. "And the chances—"

"Don't be an idiot," I hiss at him as I grab a hold and pull myself up.

He hesitates for a second before following me. It takes several minutes to climb to the top. I stop and take a look. We're amongst another sea of rocks and small hill peaks. We will be seen from another spot very easily.

Jim huffs next to me. "We don't have the fuel to keep doing this," he says.

I place a finger on my lips to keep him quiet. He's right about the fuel, but what good is reserving fuel if we're dead? The wind dies down, and we both lie on our stomachs to keep a low profile. We need to make it to the plains. If we don't these bastards can easily ambush us. Then our rifles won't be much use.

Taking in a deep breath, I hold it and let out the air, blowing red sand in front of me. My body melds into the ground. Jim is sleeping, or at least his closed eyes make it seem like that. Perhaps he's right. Though we were lucky to find bags full of food, we don't have much more time. How many more days of walking? Even more reason to hit the plains and not bother with finding our way around rocks.

And as I think about home, the thought of holding Genevine wraps itself around me. How sweet.

My neck snaps back as I wake up and the image of Genevine kissing my lips fades into the landscape facing me. I look over to see Jim on his side, sleeping silently. It's very tempting to tuck myself up in a ball and go to sleep too. But. Something woke me up.

What?

I wasn't asleep that long. Drool is still wet on the sand. Small groups of neurons in my head are tickling my skin, trying to say something. What is it? I listen. The soundscape of silence is deeper than ever. Then we can't have pursuers. They wouldn't be so quiet for so long, would they? The smell that I associate with them is gone as well. And still the hairs on my skin stand as though to look.

A voice cracks the air, and I flinch—on the rocks below where we were just walking. Whoever it is, they're not trying to be loud, but they're not scared enough to whisper.

"You sure you saw them come this way?"

"I saw them back there. And this is the only place they could walk."

Shuffling of footsteps, the harried breathing of others catching up.

"Did you see them?"

"I just told him," a sharp and annoyed voice says. "They have to be somewhere down this route."

"They're moving pretty fast. Maybe they still think we're following them."

"No. I think they're just trying to make it home. They're cowards. What do you expect?"

"Those cowards killed fifteen of us. Remember that."

"They did it when we couldn't fight. They broke the rules and slaughtered us when our weapons were down. You saw how scared they were of us."

"Yeah, they're cowards."

"We need those guns. We're not stopping until we get those guns."

"And find out where the rest of them are. I want to destroy them," a gruff voice sounds out above the chorus.

"What if they're hiding somewhere up there?"

"They don't have much food. The dumbest thing they could do is sit somewhere. Then we can just wait them out."

"All right," an older voice says, along with the dragging of a stick. "Keep it down. We've got to find them first. If there's nothing at the end of this route we'll split and search even harder."

Footsteps sound out for a few seconds, then disappear and the sound of nothing outside, and my heart pressing against my ribcage inside, fill my head.

"Christ," Jim says. "We're fucked," he says.

I wonder if they could really take on the compound. Even if only fifteen have been killed, that leaves thirty-odd left. Our compound would stand, wouldn't it? The honorable thing, I'm thinking, will be to kill ourselves and make sure that they don't get any of the information. The thought of dying kicks my brain into gear.

"We just have to be careful," I say. We're facing each other, close enough that I can smell his decaying breath.

"Dammit," he says. His eyes dart about, and etched on his face, besides those wrinkles, are the distinct fears of an old man who doesn't want to die.

"Listen to me," I say, making sure that I'm talking into his ear. "We're going to get out of here. We have to make it to the plains." I try to fend off his fear. It's infectious. "You sure about the way we're going?"

He shakes his head.

"Well, we'll have to figure it out," I say. "We will."

We make sure all our guns are loaded. I have enough for two rounds of fighting. Jim has about two and a half magazines.

"Save one for yourself," I say.

"All right," he replies.

"We'll be careful. But we have to get back before they do."

Jim cocks his head. "You think they're going to find the other set of tire tracks?"

"Yes," I say, hoping it will provide fuel for him and me. Now all I have to do is believe. After all, it wasn't too long ago when we both agreed that John was to blame for not wanting peace. Right now all the wanting in the world isn't going to help us.

We climb down the other side of the rock we're on. In a narrow gully, we walk. Jim's behind me. He makes sure to look behind us every few seconds. I look up on the rocks above us. If they've already split to look for us, and are above us, we're dead.

I try not to think about that, but my hands are sweaty. It will be dark soon. I wonder if they'll keep hunting us through the night. Is our only recourse to kill every single one of them?

My mind races, trying to keep an eye on every bend, hoping that there isn't someone waiting, and at the same time it focuses on how to kill these men. Thirty men. We don't have enough bullets, and we don't have any grenades. Even on the plains we won't stand a chance if they rush us and finish us as soon as we're out of bullets.

I stop. It has to be here.

Jim bumps into me. "What is it?" he whispers.

I feel his breath on my ear. "We have to fight them now. Ambush them."

"All of them, are you crazy?" he says, his eyes bouncing off all the rocks around us.

"We can make those traps, couldn't we?"

"Digging's too loud," he says.

Anger rises and I grab his shoulders. "Listen. We have to fight them here."

It takes a few rounds of discussions to convince Jim.

We find some soft sand and a perfect escape route.

"If they're behind us at any point, we might as well shoot ourselves," Jim says.

He's right.

We dig the soft sand up and make a trap with pointed stakes, covered with a small tarp, topped off with sand. A narrow gully will be our escape route. In it, we'll only have to fight one man at a time. Unless they have the high ground. Then we're done for. The plan is to cull their numbers some more, then run at night. There'll be no stopping this time.

The day is already half over. With the trap set, I nod to Jim and climb up a set of rocks. I'll be the lookout for the initial phase. My muscles tremble as I make it to the top. Maybe this isn't such a good idea. I feel my bladder fill up and press against my stomach. Steady. I look around from my perch. No movement as far as I can see. Further down the rocks cede to the plains. And I see the familiar landscape of the desert. It will take a few seconds for me to climb back down.

Jim starts to bang two rocks together. The cracking noise echoes off the rocks. I'm not feeling well, more like I'm more than willing to just run back home, as fast as possible. I clench my teeth trying to summon some level of anger and nerve. Funny how it seems like the more I face down someone for the prize of life, the more I see my chances fall towards zero. I thought men hardened after war.

And nothing happens. The soundscape seems to quiet down even more. After a few more seconds of Jim yelling and banging the rock, I'm certain that they're laying in ambush somewhere else. I shake my head at Jim's inquisitive look. He gives me a signal to indicate that we should wait. I don't want to. My muscles start crawling off my bones, and I have to tetanus-tense up to stay up on that rock.

Any minute now an arrow could come flying through the air. A minute after that I'll be food. Jim yells again. I try to bide the time by counting my heart beats. At least the extra blood flowing to my head increases my vision and hearing. No movement anywhere. I scan the peaks around us. Nothing. I'm breathing through my nose, but the wind's not helping our case. How did I come up with this idea? Any longer and I'm certain they'll zero in on our location and surround us. Then we'll be a few moments away from their intestinal tracts.

Jim looks up again; he's shaking his head. I'm having flashbacks to how our previous daylight ambush turned out. My muscles win out and I hop from rock to rock down to Jim.

His face is drained of blood.

"Abort," I say.

"They know what we're doing. They've always known what we're up to," Jim says in a quiet whisper.

His eyes rest somewhere off my face. I turn and look. Nothing.

"What is it?"

He nods. "Let's get the fuck outta here."

"Fine," I say. "Let's get to the plains and run until we drop."

We cut at a perpendicular angle from the narrow gully we were going to lure our pursuers up. And we run. As fast as we can. I don't care about the blind corners as I run, my handgun in one hand, and rifle slung over my shoulder.

At one point I can see the rock I was just standing on. They could've seen me for miles. What a fool I am.

I hear Jim stumble, and I turn to help him up. "You good?"

His eyes look at me, and he's in the middle of a nod, when his eyes widen by the slightest of margins. My heart flinches. I turn to see where he's looking.

Three men stand before us, holding axes. I have my handgun in hand, but I'm not thinking straight. My eyes dart to a couple rocks above us, nothing. The men are large; I didn't notice that before. I'd say more than two hundred pounds. That they can keep such weight on them, is impressive. Their size, however, isn't what's sending my balls back up my stomach. It's the look in their eyes. They have revenge on their minds, for certain, but there's a few lick of the lips that show how hungry they are. They're looking at us like we're a good meal. Remember Jenny, I remind myself. This is for her. I'm not sure how that thought drifted into my mind, but it fills me with energy.

"When I say," I say. "Start shooting."

The men are ten feet away right now. They step forward.

"Scared?" the largest one asks Jim. They all chuckle, grunt and show their teeth.

I know what to do. "Please, sir, we're friends, please don't hurt us," I hear myself say.

"Of course, come here, boy," the larger one says. The quickness with which his ax hand raises shocks me. Luckily the thought to dive and shoot is traveling through my nervous system. I dive and I hear Jim shoot. The man with the ax goes flying back. The ax leaves his hand, though with less velocity than I imagine he intended. It lands, still with impressive force, between Jim and I.

I raise my handgun and fire at the man on the left. Jim fires again. Both remaining men fall, twitching. I grab the ax between us. I hear some yells.

"Climb that way," Jim says. "There'll be more behind them."

I climb after he does and see a man run around the corner, stumbling over one of the corpses. I make it to the top of the rock and throw the ax at him. The handle hits him, though he falls. I follow Jim.

We're on a streambed with rocks, chest high, on either side again. I move my legs; my lungs burn. Every turn I expect to see a group of them with arrows drawn. This helps me run harder. The streambed leads downhill.

Off the rocks echoes of hoots and yells bounce around. I wish we had grenades.

Ten minutes later, we run into the flat land. Jim keeps running. I'm surprised that the old man has it in him.

I turn every few seconds to see if they're behind us. I can't believe that they're not. Soon we're at least half a mile from the plains. Jim stops.

"I think we got them," I say, and laugh. "Good shot, by the way."

He grins. "Let's keep walking. I can't believe our luck."

I look at the maze of rocks we just escaped. "They can still see us, if they look."

Jim chuckles. "Let them come. We'll kill a few of them."

"I've never been looked at as a meal before."

We chuckle. I notice an old soda can half wedged in the sand. I stare at it. It seems to foreign. The branding on the side has been wiped off by time. It shines, and I pick it up. I smell the inside and can almost taste cola. My stomach rumbles. I crush it and throw it down.

We walk. I hear yelps coming from the rocks. But no figures appear. What if they come at us all once? I pick up my pace to a shuffle. It's the fastest I can go without collapsing. The plain we're on is wide and only in front of us do I see more hills. On each side the world curves away from us. A mirage glimmers in the distance.

The pile of rocks we just left recedes until I can hold up a hand to cover it up. There's no way they'll try to outflank us, we'll see them. I grin at Jim, feeling invincible. "I think we're out of range. I think we're good."

Jim turns to examine our trail. "They can always follow us. Though it may take some time to find these tracks."

The sun is setting, and with that our chances of getting away increase. I look again at the place we evaded death. There's no movement.

As my thoughts travel back to Genevine, Rusty, and dealing with John, my body relaxes. My mind loats and I pinch myself just to fight off sleeping.

A gentle whisper reaches my ear. It's a roar, really, but the distance makes it seem ethereal.

Jim snaps his head. "We have a head start," he says; his eyes droop. The sun has sparked the sky again, and I don't care about another feast for my eyes. I can't see movement near the hill of rocks, not at this distance. There is, however, a reflection off the base of the rocks.

"Is that a mirage?" I ask as the image wavers in front of me.

"No. That's their axes."

It takes me a moment to realize that the reason it seems like the ripple of a sea, is because they're all running in unison. Another roar whispers in my ear. This time it's a half-notch louder.

My body secretes adrenaline into my body. The jolt travels around me. Instead of power coursing through my veins, I feel my muscles rebel with pain. Tears almost form, and I almost collapse.

"Come on," Jim says and tugs my arm.

I follow him in our shuffle, which quickly turns into a fast jog after the next roar.

Jim is looking ahead at the peaks in the horizon with renewed intensity. I stare ahead.

"Recognize that?" Jim says, with a smirk.

I squint. The sun has fallen through the horizon and left the land with only shards of light, that filter between objects, blurring them beyond recognition. "I don't see it," I say. All I make out are the exclamation points of hills I'm sure I've never climbed.

"That's near home. No more than a mile," Jim says, his voice highlighted with sunshine.

I feel energy pouring into my body. The arteries in my head pound a few drumbeats. "You certain?" I ask. I don't care about the truth; I just want him to say it's true.

"Damn certain," he says.

I try to make a map in my head to see how far those hills are. They surely can't be that far away, can they?

We jog, a fast shuffle, and I feel like my body's floating. We keep at it, shuffling along, dodging the holes in the dark, never stumbling. We can't see the men behind us, now, but I can't hear them either. We're still leaving tracks, so I imagine that they're following us.

A shriek of pain runs up my leg. We're traveling over hard flat rock. It's odd terrain, and that thought is only briefly entertained by my focused mind.

"Stop," Jim says.

I don't want to, of course, because this light feeling, almost a touch of drunk, threatens to fold back to pain if I do. I stop. "What is it?"

"Run a few steps forward, then run back in your steps," he says.

He runs forward, and I follow him. We run where the ground is soft. He stops and tracks back, carefully. I sniff the air. Only some sulfuric gas from Jim. It's quiet, except the crunches of our shoes. My mind can't help but think that something is wrong, that any second now the cannibals will come screaming out of the dark, and we won't do anything except suck-start our own guns as they overrun us.

We backtrack to the hard ground, and he takes off at a perpendicular angle.

"I learned this in the military," he says. I can see his teeth when he smiles, and I smell something like rotting cheese.

When we step into soft ground again, he turns, moving backwards, and rubs out his tracks. I do the same. It seems to do the job, unless someone looks closely, at least.

Jim does this for much too long. We turn, and at a slight angle from our original trajectory, we head off running.

"Aim for that peak there," he says, pointing at a rock that looks something like a crow. I return to the shuffle, staring at the ground in front of me as it morphs from the darkness into shapes my mind makes up.

Dark shadows. Place foot here. Over and over.

"You keeping track of the rock?" Jim asks.

I look up. The hills seem to have changed. I squint. They're closer. "That one, right?" I say as Jim leans in to me.

"That's right," he says. "Keep an eye on it, or else we'll lose it."

I try to make an effort, but my eyes drop to the ground as soon as I stop thinking about it.

I zone out.

After what seems to be an eternity, Jim swears.

"What?" I ask.

"Do you see it?"

The hills and rocks are closer now. I'm sure we're less than a mile away, but I can't see the crow's peak. "Me either."

Jim's breathing hard.

"What's the difference? Let's head to the hills. You said you said you knew them, right?"

"I knew that peak. The rest of them I'm not sure. The range is long. You understand that, right?" he says, anger and exhaustion lace his voice. "If we stray off, not only will we possibly be caught again, but we'll be even further from home."

I hadn't thought about that. And as the bottom falls out of my hope, I wonder why I hadn't paid attention. Will it be this last mistake that gets us killed? Blood runs from my head. I feel light-headed.

For a second I'd been thinking that all this luck was really guidance from Him talking to me, testing me. A more insidious thought runs through me: all men who were defeated thought this way. That the luck that brought them as far as it did was God. But what did they feel the moment before they died?

I try to stare at the shapes in front of us. We walk forward for a few minutes.

"There," I say, a relief rippling through my body. It's as clear as day. I feel the guidance of His hand.

We break out into a shuffle and in no less than an hour we're at the base of the hill.

"You recognize this?" I ask.

"We've to climb over. Can't lose our bearings when we get in there, though."

There are too many clouds to help us. We start climbing the rocks. Before the plains disappear I take a last glance at them. Dark, quiet. Where are those men? The stillness of the land flicks odd thoughts into my head. They crawl, these thoughts, and wrap tight around my head. Man was never meant to be alone. And if they are alone in nothingness like this, one can only deem what they experience as madness.

We climb over the spine of the hills and are soon heading on a downhill trajectory. I stumble, my muscles too weak to slow me down. Jim stumbles. I stumble again, tearing skin off my knees and palms. Jim falls. I hear the crunch of his bones, and he develops a limp. We hold hands to better balance ourselves. We're going slow now. Very slow.

Threads of lights simmer on the horizon. We take careful steps. I breath through my nose, trying to sense if the men are anywhere near us.

Something twinkles in the corner of my eye. I snap my neck trying to catch it. It's gone.

I tap Jim. "Did you see that?" I point in the general direction.

His eyes narrow as he tries to make out what I saw.

"I'm sure it..." I decide to let it be. It could be spots in my eyes, or a tired mind falling apart. We take care with our steps, and I see the flash again. I look up. Nothing. I move my eyes around, seeing if I can mimic the effect. Nothing. Then it appears again.

"Jim, look, there," I say. It's the slow flicker of a distant light. Manmade light.

"There," I say again, tugging his shoulder. I hope he sees it because otherwise I'm sure I've lost it.

"I don't see nothing," he says to me and scrunches his face up at me.

I try to focus on the ground as we make it down. The rocks seem to be harder than ever. I shift the weight to different parts of my feet, but every bone in my body feels shattered. When we touch the ground and are met with soft dirt, I let out a sigh of relief. The shadows disappear and Jim points at two peaks that look like a camel's back. "That way," he says.

"Are you sure?" I ask, if that's where the compound is, then we're a long way off.

"Of course I am," he says. His voice is cracking.

We break out into a shuffle. It takes several minutes before my joints loosen up for the movement. My muscles are just as hurt, and the feeling of glass cutting through them doesn't stop until later, when the glass melts and leaves heat in its wake. Our speed is pathetic, and we realize this simultaneously and break out into a fast walk. I glance back, hoping we're specks by the time the day falls.

"We're a damn sad sight," Jim says, glancing at me with a smile. "If they come over that hill now, and see us, and have the energy to run, we might be done," he says.

I nod. Too many close calls to care. That's a lie; if they come over that hill I think I'll find a way to push off the pain to fight. As if to disagree, my back convulses, and I twist it to knead out the knots. "Only a couple more miles," I say.

"Only a few," he says.

How long will that take us? Another glance at the hills; the tension of fear dwells in my heart, as I pray not to see those axes in the morning sun. Still no movement.

"Crazy thing, this desert," Jim says. "It's something odd that the previous civilization came from the desert. The ideas and thoughts all came from there. God, too." His tongue flashes out and I see that his lips are red with cracks, and he gags as he tries to swallow. "We need water," he says when he catches me staring at his lips.

I try to lick my own lips. He's right. We need water. I taste the blood from the cracks of my lips.

"God spoke to people only in the desert. But I don't see why," Jim said.

He's dancing around the ideas that MacGee had.

"Why not?" I ask. I want him to be more like MacGee.

"I mean…" His eyes lock into mine for a few seconds. He scans my irises. "There's no God now, and there's a damn reason for that. People who say they talk to God are the Johns of this world. They know how to lie to others, and can do it without breaking a sweat."

"Then there's those people who can't lie too well. They have to build up their reserves to lie. They need that time alone to build up their lies."

"What do you mean?"

Jim huffs. "I mean that they do something that they know others aren't likely to do, so it gives them some power... they use the time alone in the desert to make things up."

That heretic talk makes me turn again, as if it could be a cue to the men following us. Nothing. The rocks are getting smaller, though not fast enough for my tastes. "The desert has mysterious ways," I say, and feel immediately foolish for doing so. The crunch sound of our steps fills my head.

"Nothing good ever came out of land like this," he says.

"John…" I say in return, thinking about our previous ideas. "Maybe peace isn't it."

That precipitates a strong silence.

"You're probably right," I say. Not feeling like looking at Jim, I glance over my shoulder at the rocks. Nothing. The sun's bright, fragments of clouds vaporize before it. What Jim said makes sense, but I'm scared of it.

"If we don't make it through this, it won't matter," he says.

Not wanting to be the reason he stopped, I wait for more. Perhaps I'll have to prod him. We're about a few miles from the crow's peak when a whisper-roar sounds. We both freeze, then spin.

The movement is once again obvious. They're where we were, so they must not have been fooled all that much by Jim's backtracking.

"Here they come," Jim says.

The movement of the men is beautiful at this time of day. And my brain slowly makes the connection: matching their up and down movements with my repertoire of what a man looks like when he's running. Fast. How could they have that much energy?

"Damn bastards," Jim says. "They're going to beat us, aren't they?"

His voice sounds more matter of fact than resigned.

"We can jog," I say. "Before the sun gets too high." I know that's not the way it will turn out. For some reason those men have all the energy in the world. "How long do you think it will take for them to get here?"

"At that rate they'll take over us in a few minutes."

I judge how far away the camel's peak is. Less than a mile. "Screw them. Let's run to the rocks."

We jog. Only for a few minutes, then we walk fast. My muscles feel like they're rusted on my bones and would rather not move at all.

I look back. The men have gone silent, but they are still moving, albeit slower, and their outlines are larger.

"You're wrong about John," Jim says.

"What?"

"There *is* peace, and this would never have happened if John hadn't sent us. Mitt and Craig would still be here. Whatever happens here, don't forget that."

"We're both getting out of this. Dead or alive."

"I thought you were smarter than that. I thought you were one of the leaders," he says. He seems to be mocking me. Perhaps Jim was made to be mad—like MacGee.

A shard strikes my heart.

I pick up my pace. We reach the feet of the camel peaks, every shred of energy burned under the sun. My breaths are shallow. I turn to see how close the men are. I can make out their strands of hair bouncing with their strides, and their eyes flash here and there. Maybe less than a mile.

Jim turns and pulls out his rifle. "You ready for this?"

"We can keep going," I say. "I'm sure we're not that far from the compound. I'm holding on to the hope that the light I saw earlier in the morning was something, and not a hallucination."

"You can keep going," Jim says. "I'm going to stay here." He doesn't look at me.

I don't have the energy to argue. My mind duels with itself. Go back to Genevine. You'll find more peace there than any talk with Jim.

"You're a fool," I say with as much anger as possible.

Jim is aiming down his rifle. The men, at least twenty, are jogging towards us, shuffling more like it, but they're getting bigger, though I wouldn't say that they're within shooting range yet. Not in our state.

"I'm going to take as many of them out as I can."

131

I grit my teeth and try to think of something that will work on him. I'm not leaving him. He might be the only friend I have. "You just said nothing good ever came out of a desert, right?" I say.

He's squinting through one eye down his rifle.

"Right?" I speak louder.

"And what does that mean, smart man?"

"Well don't be a weakling and let them have at you," I say. "Craig and Mitt would love that. Love knowing that they died so you could give up."

His head rises from the rifle. "You piece of shit."

"So go ahead, give up," I say and turn. I hear him come after me. I'm not sure if he's following or chasing, so I stay a good healthy distance away. We climb until we get to a good vantage point. I turn and look at the men. Half a mile away. They all look ragged. Whatever gave them their energy before, it's all gone now. They're shuffling. Are they really that bent on killing us? I count them out. Twenty.

"Screw this," Jim says and lies down with his rifle. He shoots, and I watch as a man tumbles forward, his momentum sprays up sand. He fires again. Another man falls over. The others start to run back. They must know what our range is.

I lie down and start shooting. We won't get a better chance than this.

"Two left," Jim says.

I fire at one man brave enough not to run too far back. I don't see him react. He turns, then collapses. "I have two left," I say. The rest are in my handgun.

Jim yelps. "See? Look at them run," he says.

"Wait," I say. The men are far back now. They're lying down.

I watch as more run back. I wait for a mistake.

"What did you do in the military?"

The men are moving perpendicular to our position, though they do so with measured steps.

"Grunt," he says.

"Army?"

"Does it matter?"

"You scared of your past?" I say.

"Weren't *you?*"

Why am I being so confrontational? Besides, should we be fighting? The enemy is right there in front of us.

"Yes. I was," I say.

"What are you going to do about John?" he asks.

"Let's get back first."

The men are coming back at us. We shift our position and fire at the closest ones. Jim hits him in the thigh. He tumbles and lets out a wail. His friends turn and run. This time they go further back. That's what we needed.

"Great shot," I say.

"Lucky," he says. We watch them pull back and move at another perpendicular angle from us. We slide back and when we're out of sight head the way I saw the light. I can smell a powerful ammonia smell wafting off my muscles. I feel like I'm receding further back into my skull. Any more of this and we will surely be finished. How many days can the human body survive without water?

"You're with me, aren't you?" I ask.

An hour later I see the outline of our gates. Behind us is the dusty desert landscape, punctuated by rocks. We walk. Every step threatens to shatter my body.

At the gates I see commotion amongst the guards. The gates open a crack and a several men walk out. Neither I nor Jim have the moisture in our throats to yell. We wave our hands and throw down our guns. The men come up to us.

"It's Tom and Jim," one of them says.

I can't recognize them. "Don't separate us," I say. They look at me confused. "Water," I say. They pour water from a canteen into my mouth. It hurts at first, burns, then the coolness sends what mimics an orgasm through my body, and I let out a gurgle.

"Go get John," I hear a gruff voice say. It doesn't sound friendly, or happy to see us.

I forgot the dangers that lay here. "Don't separate us," I say. But they don't listen.

I point from where we came. "Men, chasing us."

"Where?"

"A mile back. Fifteen of them."

I fade out as the sky passes above me.

I open my eyes. When I try to move my head to see what's next to me, I feel the cuts of a hundred knives all over my body. The pain takes me by surprise and I gasp, moan; it feels like it actually might win out, that the pain will tear me apart, limb from limb.

"Tom?" a voice from another room sounds off. Who is that?

I try to say that I want something to eat, some water, but what comes out is another gasp. I'm sure that I'm in my room, though I'm not a hundred percent certain.

A shadow moves across the room, and I see a hand touch my head.

"His fever is gone."

"Rusty?" I manage to say, though the words act like blades on my vocal chords.

"Hi, Tom."

Another figure appears behind her. "Tom," the voice says, cold, maybe hurt.

"Genevine?" I ask.

She sits next to me and takes my hand. I gasp at the movement.

"Sorry," she says.

Rusty leans into my ear. "She's still angry."

I try to think why and I remember. "Ge…" I say and collapse.

I wake up to see Genevine, Rusty and another person I don't recognize standing above me.

"Tom. How are you?"

I shift my head, preparing for extreme pain. But it's subdued now, so I try to sit up.

"Easy there. We're giving you meds for the pain, but you should take it slow."

I nod, and the room takes a few seconds to shift with my eyeballs. "Jim?"

"Jim is fine. He's in another building. You two are something else," the man says.

"You?"

"I'm the doctor. Officially now. Jim had to be brought back from life. You're younger. You should be fine in no time. The old man will take longer."

Something in my brain tells me that this is an issue, but I don't say anything. I wonder where John is. "The men. Chasing," I say.

"Oh, that..." the doctor says and looks up at Genevine and Rusty. "They didn't find anyone. Or anything."

"Tracks," I say.

"None."

"John."

"He'll be here when you're ready."

I feel like his voice says I'm in trouble.

"Get some rest," he says.

I wake up once more, and the room's dark. I scratch my face, my crotch. Some pain lingers, but it's bearable. I sit up and reach over, expecting to see Genevine. She's not there. That feeling in my stomach is gone.

My bladder shrieks. That's why I woke up. I get up and walk myself to the bathroom. I lean against the wall as I urinate. Jim. I need to find him. If they didn't find any trace of the cannibals, does that mean our pursuers gave up? That knot in my stomach, the one that I couldn't interpret is back.

I check the other rooms, hoping to see someone. The one across from me has Genevine and Rusty sleeping together. They seem like mother and daughter, these two. I'm hit with a wall of sadness, at knowing that they chose to sleep in a separate room.

I try to shake off my melancholy, but it lingers. I peek my head out the front door. It's nighttime and everything is quiet. Our long journey is over and seems like a dream. Did we really come that close to death?

I close my eyes back on my bed. Sleep doesn't come. Images and emotions swirl inside my head and make a heady cocktail. A voice sounds up. I'm no longer in my room, but in that dusty shack with MacGee.

What do you want? I ask

He stares at me.

I can't really see him, but from the smell I know it's him.

Are you judging me? I ask.

You killed me.

It would have been worse. I say instinctively.

He lets out a horrid cough.

You were supposed to help.

I feel that knot in my stomach. Insurmountable guilt. It eats away at me.

What could I have done? I yell.

You did nothing to help me.

I tried to get you a trial. I... I stop talking. I always thought that those things were done to help him, but hearing them makes them sound like the opposite.

Was it the same with that girl? MacGee asks.

Did I ever tell him?

Jenny. The reason she's dead is me.

Was it? MacGee asks.

It was. I say and feel a lightness in my heart that doesn't seem right.

And the life you lived before this, how was that? he asks.

I was a better man back then; I knew how to be good and to give. I say.

You were always the same man. MacGee says, coughs.

I've done so much since.

You have.

I feel his hand on mine.

I'm sorry MacGee. You were a friend. I should have done more.

He doesn't answer.

MacGee? Did you hear me?

I wake up to see Genevine shaking me.

"You're having a nightmare," she says.

I'm drenched in sweat. "Is it morning?" I ask.

"What was the dream about?"

"Nothing," I say.

She doesn't take my hand, or lean in to touch me. She's looking at me like a stranger would. That cuts deep. I want her warmth next to me again. I want to feel her lips on mine. She's too angry for any of that.

"I'm sorry," I say. "Sorry for what I did to you. For leaving you."

She doesn't react.

"I had a premonition that something bad was going to happen to the scouts. That they might die. I was sure it was God talking. So I went out with them." I study her face for any sort of tell. She's staring into my eyes, but her face is stolid. I know it's a lie, and that in fact I know nothing about God's works. But I feel better for saying it, so I keep going. "I was right. We were ambushed. Mitt and Craig died. Jim and I barely escaped with our lives."

Still nothing.

Rusty peeks her head in and disappears just as quickly.

"I thought I was going to die. They chased us over the desert for days," I say.

She leans in.

"And you know the only thing I could think about? Was holding you in my arms," I say.

"Really?" she asks, her face not believing me.

"Yes," I say.

I feel her hand on mine, and my heart glows warm as she kisses me.

"I missed you," she said. "I was sure you were dead. Everyone here thought that."

"The doctor said they didn't find any evidence of the cannibals, that true?" I ask.

"True, people have been wondering what happened. Jim is out, and might not be a hundred percent ever again."

That's not good. I need Jim. "Have they said anything else about me?"

"People just want you to get better," she says and strokes my hair. She lies done next to me.

"I mean John and the council," I say.

"Oh, them. They've been quiet. The trucks are quiet again. I heard them asking what happened to the scout's truck."

"Destroyed," I say.

Rusty comes in the room with a tray full of food. "Here you go," she says.

I eat it, taking only moments to taste it. Eggs, mixed with some sort of flour. There's water to wash it down. "Has the food shortage been figured out?" I ask.

Genevine shakes her head. "Not yet."

"What did they say?" I ask, though all these issues seem mundane and important at the same time.

"Nothing, so far."

I finish the rest of my meal. "You two eat?"

"Yes, we're good," Rusty says.

All the fire that previously resided in her eyes has disappeared. I'm disappointed by that. "And you, what have you been up to? Getting used to this place?"

She smiles and glances at Genevine.

"Rusty was being picked on by the other kids at school. She got into a few fights. They wanted her out. So I decided to home school her."

"Oh." How long have I been out? I decide not to ask. "And how do you like that?" I ask her.

She nods her head and buries it in my chest. I pat her back. "Don't worry about them. You just concentrate and learn as much as you can. We'll teach you everything," I say. But what do I teach her? And if the world is divided into people like us, who attack and kill the likes of Thomas, as well as the likes of the cannibals, what world was I preparing her for?

"Can you teach me to shoot?" Rusty asks.

"I said you would," Genevine says.

"Everyone says you're the best shot here. You and Jim."

I don't know what we'll do for bullets. I don't even know if I have the energy for that, but I agree.

"I want to see Jim," I say.

"I think John said he wants to talk to you as soon as you're up," Genevine says. Rusty and Genevine exchange looks.

That thought of John controlling my movements, angers me. "Take me to Jim."

I walk, though it's in shuffles. On either side, Rusty and Genevine hold my hands. The day is well on its way to being half over, and people stare at me. There isn't a mirror to see what I look like. "Do I look pretty rough?" I ask.

"Yes," Genevine says. Then caresses my face. "Don't worry, I still like you." She smiles at Rusty, who grins at me, as if they're sharing a joke. It should be a moment for me to laugh, to enjoy seeing sunshine on the faces of the only two women left in my life, but my brain doesn't allow that. Instead, it thinks about the possibility that in the past few days John might have gotten to these two women, and they could be his eyes and ears.

We walk to a shack on the other side of the compound. There's a guard at the door.

"Why's there a guard?" I whisper to Genevine.

She shrugs. "Why not?"

I'm annoyed with her attitude, though when Rusty squeezes my hand, I decide to let it go.

"What business do you have here?" the young man says.

I glance him up and down. I could take him, but I won't in my current condition. "Jim in there?" I ask.

He narrows his eyes at me. "Who are you?"

"Tom," I say.

"Oh," he says. "I'm sorry. I'm not allowed to let anyone in here. Except the doctor and John."

"Well, you're letting me in," I say. I reach down for my handgun, and realize that I didn't bring it.

Genevine steps forward. "You're going to tell a hero that he can't see his friend?"

The young man thinks about it, then steps back. "Sorry."

I walk in. The room smells like old blood and feces. I hear the rusty breathing of Jim. His face is peaceful, but not in a good way. He's pale, like permanent shock.

"Jim," I say as I stroke his head. His head's cool to the touch. "Jim." I say again, this time closer to his ear. He stirs, but still breathes like a man sleeping for his life.

"I don't think he can hear you," Genevine says.

"Wait outside," I say. "Let me know if someone wants to get in."

They leave, and I lock the door and sit down on the bed next to Jim. He opens his eyes.

"Faking it, eh?" I say and grin. Whatever differences arose out on that plain, running from those madmen, it's all gone now.

He grins back at me. "Of course. You think I want to talk to these bastards?"

I look around, nervous that someone might be in here. But it's only a room, with dusty walls and floors, and a small table next to the bed. "You hear them say anything?"

"They don't know what happened to us, so they're scared. They're dying to hear it from us."

"John come by?"

"He sounded scared." Jim grins. I pat him.

"You going to gain your strength back?" I ask.

"It's back."

"Try and walk first," I say, rubbing my knees.

"Aw... You hurt?" he asks in an ironic tone.

"Fuck you," I say, and we chuckle.

"I thought at one point that everything was over. That the story that was Jim was going to finally be in some barbarian's shit."

"You should be so lucky," I say.

"You bastard."

I'm at peace here, with my friend. I think about Genevine's looks and somewhat cold demeanor. "I don't know about Genevine."

"The wifey?"

"She seems off."

"Cause you left her on your wedding day to hang out with men. What would you think?"

He has a point. I remember my dream with MacGee. I also think about the barbarians who just tried to kill us. I wonder if perhaps John might not be so bad when compared with them. MacGee battles that thought out of my mind.

I have a friend in Jim now, and I know what I have to do. "What you said in the desert…" I watch him for any reactions.

"I meant it," he says, defensively.

"Good," I pat his hand. "You're going to have to round up some troops. Gather the ones you can trust, and the ones that will fall behind. We'll get an inner and outer circle."

He smiles. "I knew you would say that. Smart bastard, you are," he says.

"It'll take time," I say, trying to soothe some of the tension that's creeping up my spine. For a split second I entertain the thought that I might end up in that chair in that room, men tearing me to pieces.

"Don't back out," Jim growls. "Time is only an excuse to change your mind."

"Get on it, then," I say, surprised.

A loud knock sounds. "Tom? Open up."

"Your girlfriend is here," Jim says.

"I'm coming!" I yell. It's John. "You ready for this?" I ask Jim.

"I am." He grabs my wrist. "Tom. He can sense these things."

"I know," I say. I get up and walk to the door. Why did Jim say that? I take a deep breath. Don't waver. Love him. Like a brother.

I open the door. John and several other guards stand before me. The look on John's face is hard. I throw open my arms. "John," I say, trying to force tears, or at least a wet eye. "It's so good to see you brother." I embrace him and it takes a second before he hugs me back.

"I thought you were going to shoot him," John says with a grin as he nods at Jim.

"No. Just two men laughing at our luck." I shake my head. "Do we have a story to tell you."

"Well," John says, the authoritative timbre returning to his voice. "That's exactly why I'm here."

"I heard no sign of the barbarians were found?" I ask.

"That's right."

"You followed our tracks?" I ask.

"Well…"

"Not to worry," I say, trying to be as nice as possible. "We'll show ya'll. Two of you, help Jim up. We'll talk in the main hall?"

"That's great," John says. I can see his eyes are somewhat confused. I need to be nice, but not too nice.

I make sure I walk with Jim near me.

"How's the food problem?" I ask.

John leans in to whisper. "I'll tell you more after."

"Of course," I say. There's something about him. He doesn't trust me.

In the main hall we're seated in front of the council and John. About half the people from the flock stand behind us to listen. I start out with my version of the events, highlighting what Jim did. I get about halfway, and I take a deep breath. Everyone's leaning in, waiting for what I'll say next. My mind runs away from me and throws those words of wisdom Jim said about the desert. Surely *something* good will come out of it.

"And as we were walking in the night, and I was certain it was my last night on earth. Dead certain. I saw a light. I thought it was a star. But it got larger and larger. Suddenly I couldn't stare at it. And as this light took over me, I felt warm all over. And a voice comes to me. It was… and I know this sounds out there… but it was God. Funny," I say and look at my hands. I gather my strength and look up at the council, John. "You never know what it feels like until it happens to you. But He was talking to me and He told me to go on. Never give up. He said to carry out His works." Everyone around me is nodding.

"That's right," Jim says. "I saw the light, but it came at him. I could see it, though I couldn't believe it. I thought we were dead too, and that night we found strength from above and moved on."

The last word Jim speaks echoes off the walls until it's a whine in my ear. Jim nods, and he looks at me with a gruff approval. I try to smile at John, hoping it comes across as a brave, tired smile, all the while thinking about MacGee. What John made me do to my friend.

"Well it sounds like you two are heroes," John says. The men of the council agree, and a round of approving murmurs rises up from the crowd.

"May I say that Mitt and Craig are of the first order of heroes," I say.

"I don't think anyone will argue that," John says. He looks at the council members, and they all nod their heads.

"And I think Jim here deserves a promotion. His tactical and strategic ability was second to none."

John seems a little more uncomfortable at this proposition. But the crowd mutters its approval. John looks at the council members, and they nod. "And I don't think anyone could possibly disagree with that," he says. He raises his hand for the crowd to be silent.

"Then there's the matter of these barbarians," John says.

"That's right," Jim speaks up. "We'll show you where to look, but my guess is that they've left. We whipped them pretty bad with the Lord's hand."

The crowd laughs and a couple of hands clap.

"The question is," John says, annoyed. "How do we defeat them?"

I'm not sure what to say, and John is staring right at me. There hasn't been much time to think this out. Is John trying to knock me down a notch? Besides, I can't very well mention peace after the story I told, where the Mitt and Craig are eaten, can I?

"For now, I recommend we keep patrols in the near area. We can think of the final war in the next few days," Jim says.

"Think about it we must," John says. His head is drifting which means that he's thinking about something really hard. "The Lord's people cannot be spit upon like this without repercussions."

The crowd hails this statement with claps and cheers. I nod my head and stick out my chest, trying to seem as tough as possible.

When the meeting adjourns, the crowd envelops us and thanks us, gushing over us. Asking about God. I shake hands, smile and nod up at the sky. I see Samantha in the crowd with her James. She flashes me a smile. I smile back. There's no harm, is there?

Jim and I take a truck with John and some other soldiers. We try to retrace our steps. It takes an hour to find them. The soil is yellow in places, but there are no bones. I see the disbelief on everyone's faces. Jim gives me a shrug. Then John sees a mound. We dig it up and see nothing but bones.

"The insects must have gotten them," John says.

"No," I say. "These bastards eat their own."

After we get back, a crowd of people are still waiting for us. They engulf the truck. Some try to touch me as I step out. I shake hands again. I see Samantha in the background, but no Genevine.

"A moment?" John asks.

I follow him to his place. I smell something like victory off him, and I don't like it. There are two guards in front of the door. I wish I had my handgun. Inside we're alone, and he shuts the door. If he wanted to take me out, now would be the time. I'm the weakest I've been in a long time.

"Congratulations again on surviving," he says. There's jealousy in his voice.

"Thank you," I say. "What about the food?"

He grins. "Down to business, eh?"

"Well the Lord's Kingdom needs to survive. We must work for the Lord."

"We must," he says, eyeing me. Does he not believe my story?

"Some of the plant life we grew died with the last harvest. It looks like we might be able to salvage the next one. But the plants are growing weaker," John says.

I never asked how it was done, especially with the bad soil we have here. "Have you tried cycling them?" I ask. John gives me an odd look. "I remember a teacher mentioning that some plants take certain nutrients out and that if one didn't cycle them, the soil would be leeched of all good."

"I'm impressed. We'll look into it," John says. He seems to relax.

"It will help with the war, right?"

"That's right. It's a war that they obviously started. And besides, we can't live in a world where people eat each other."

I pause, perhaps a second too long. "Of course not," I say. John's looking at me; his eyes are slightly narrowed. "They ate Mitt and Craig. And tried to eat me." I throw some anger behind that last statement. "No one gets away with that." I stare into John's eyes. He looks away. "And whatever you want me to do. As the Lord bid me to do, I shall," I add.

That seems to drain the worry or strain from his face. "Of course. We shall do this for the Lord, shan't we?"

I try my hardest to maintain eye contact with him. I take a step towards him.

"I'm happy to see you again," I say.

John looks a little confused. He nods. "Glad you made it back all right. The place wouldn't be the same with out you."

"Thanks to the Lord," I say and we embrace.

"Indeed," John says, his face less suspicious now.

We pray together, and I lower my head as far as I can.

I get back to my house near dusk. Genevine is talking to a few women at the front door.

"Well, well," Genevine says with a sneer on her face. "If it isn't the hero."

The other women blush and melt away.

"What's gotten into you?" I ask, as I close the front door behind me.

Genevine walks to our room.

The house seems empty. "Rusty here?"

No answer. I walk into our room and see that Genevine is sitting on our bed.

"Are you going to be quiet all day?"

"Night, hero. It's nighttime."

Anger sweeps up over me.

"Are you kidding me?" I ask, shutting the bedroom door behind me. "Can't you lay off me for a second?"

She rolls her eyes. "Samantha asked about you again."

"So?" I ask. "Is that why you're mad? A woman I can't control asks after me?"

"I'm mad because I know when you lie, and you do it all the time."

I gulp. Was she there at the main hall? Did she see me when I mentioned the Light of God?

"About what?" I ask.

"There you go again."

"What do you mean?"

"I'm talking about you and Samantha."

"There's nothing between us." I hold her hand and look into her eyes.

"What? You think I'm going to fall for that?" She shakes off my hand.

She sleeps in the same bed as I, but she manages to maintain space between our bodies. I'm cold on my side, but I'm not sure what to do. All that time when I was being chased I expected to come here and be welcomed. I hoped to rest in the warmth of her body. I wonder if John did get to her.

She breathes in a slight snore. I turn away from her. If she wants to be cold, I'll do the same.

The next morning I wake up to hear cooking. I walk into the kitchen. Rusty and Genevine are in the kitchen.

"How's everyone today?" I ask.

"I'm good," Rusty says and comes over for a hug. She mouths something to me and looks over at Genevine.

I cock my head to ask what she means, but Rusty heads into her room before I can ask.

"Funny kid," I say.

Genevine doesn't say anything; she's staring at the cutting board in front of her. There's a knife in her hand. I step up to her and she turns, the knife tip touching my belly.

"What's got into you?" I ask, and regret it when I see the hurt and anger on her face.

"You are such…" she says and shakes her head, the knife pressing into my belly. Any more pressure, and she'll draw blood.

"I'm sorry," I say. "I'm sorry about what I did on our wedding. All right?"

The knife lowers a few inches, but now it's near my groin, though no longer touching me.

I hold her stare and grab a hold of her elbows. "I'm really sorry," I say. "I'll try to be better. But if you want me to leave, I will."

Her eyes glisten. The knife lowers to near my thighs now. "What about Rusty?" she asks.

Is she taking me up on my threat? It wasn't meant to be taken that way. Though I remember so many things about Jenny and Carol, for some reason I can't remember how we argued, only the moment after the arguments.

"I don't know. We can figure out something," I say, my heart dropping.

She lets the knife fall to her side, her eyes on her feet. Am I destined to destroy all love that I find? Or perhaps it's love that I saw, but never was? My heart falls into a vacuum. The other particles in my body shrivel.

"I don't want you to go," she says.

Confused, I fix my eyes on the knife. What's she thinking?

"Then what?" I ask.

Her eyes take me in with a hard-softness that cuts right to my core.

"Don't go," she says.

"I won't," I say, small threads reaching out from my heart and attaching to her voice, touch, aura.

She forces a smile. "Just don't head out like that again," she says, waving the knife in front of my face.

"Of course," I say, my head light, my heart bouncing up to my throat. All it takes is a smile from her and I'm lucid.

We embrace and I feel her breasts against my chest and the handle of the knife on my back. We kiss. She smiles. I take hold of the knife and guide it to the counter.

"Let's not fight with a knife next time," I say.

She pantomimes jabbing at me. "I need it to keep you in check."

I chuckle. "Of course you do."

"Are you guys done fighting?" Rusty asks.

She's at her doorway, a sliver of her staring at us.

"Of course, come here," Genevine says.

We start on breakfast. Rusty and Genevine's heads bounce as they eat. I feel closer to them than ever before. Closer to this compound. My verve to take on John dissipates.

"What's next?" Genevine asks.

Before I can think of an answer there's a knock.

I open the door to see Jim staring at me with black sacs of exhaustion beneath his eyes.

"You feeling better?" I ask.

He gives me a furious look and brushes past me as he walks in.

"We need to talk," he says.

Genevine's head tilts. I raise my eyebrows and bite my lip as if to say what can I do. She listens, God bless her.

"Rusty, let's finish breakfast in your room and start your studies."

Rusty doesn't complain. She looks at me as if to give me some mental help, and walks to her room, plate of fried-something in hand.

The two women disappear. Jim steps close. His decayed smell makes me immediately miss Genevine.

"John dead yet?" he asks. He almost yells it.

"Keep your voice down," I say. What's wrong with him? There're beads of sweat on his forehead, as if he's been running for some time. "Where have you come from?"

"I thought you were going to do it last night." He leans in to examine my face. "You really didn't, did you?"

"Jim, what the hell are you talking about?" I say, somewhat startled.

He mumbles to himself: "Christ. This is bad."

I take in a deep breath. "Jim. What the hell are you talking about?"

"You don't get it, do you? You don't know what you're doing, what you're up against."

A small inkling of what he might be saying tickles the extremities of my body. But if it's John he's worried about, if it's the moments back in the desert when we were being chased, and we promised each other…

"You came up with the whole Light of God thing, and I figured you knew what you were doing," he says.

I remembered that. The good that can come out of a desert. Is that why he's angry?

"And what about the light?" I say.

"You claimed to talk to God, if I remember right."

"That's right."

"And you think John will let that be? He's the one who talks to God. You just pushed in on his territory. What the hell wee you thinking?"

"We'll have the people on our side."

"These people are like people throughout time. They're sheep. They're not the ones you have to worry about. You have to worry about John. You're about to end up just like the others. The old council members who thought they could win over the people. They're dead. They thought they could be clever like you, and they were dead within hours."

My mind chews on what Jim has just said. If it's true my time is limited. That feeling in my guts grows, taking over my intestines and winding them up.

"John seemed to take it well," I say. "I talked to him at his place." My voice cracks; my throat is dry.

"And that's what he wants you to think. You're next. We're next," Jim says and punches his chest. "I'm the one who agreed to seeing the same thing that you did."

My knees weak, I sit down at the table. "All right. Well we'll go forward. I'll be quick," I say, though it sounds like a lie. I have to make sure that Jim is on my side, convince him that this will turn out all right. "I told him God said to do what he said."

Jim's face softens. "That may help," he says and sits down next to me.

"We'll have to be careful," I say. "You talk to anyone?"

Jim shakes his head. "Not yet. Wish to hell Mitt and Craig were here."

"Well we can't wish ourselves life. Besides, they would want us to avenge their deaths."

"That's true."

"All right. Get out there; find the others. I'll try to talk to others."

"Don't be too obvious," Jim says.

"I know, " I reply. "You too. Just get people on our side. Say that we need to do it for John."

"What do you plan on doing?" Jim asks.

I don't know, but there's no way I'm telling him that. "I'll get something going. Get the toughest men that you can." I think. How are we going to do this? All the people could turn against us, and then what?

Voices sound off outside, and we both freeze. I feel my belt and realize that my handgun is in my room. "Make sure you're armed at all times," I say.

"Of course," he replies.

"And find the toughest ones who are against us. Or extremely loyal to John."

"I know a couple off the top of my head."

"They work together?" I ask.

"They do.

"It'll have to be at night," I say, though I don't know where this thought came from.

"At night," Jim says, lending my idea credibility. I realize that he needs me, wants me to show him the way. Odd how useful he is in battle, yet here those tactics don't seem to help.

"By the way, if you see people who are neutral. Tell them... How much I've been changed by the Light of God."

Jim screws his face at me. "Really?"

"Do it. It will help us keep them at bay."

"I don't—"

"Do it," I say, somewhat annoyed.

More voices outside the building silence us. The way our breathing crystalizes, makes it apparent how dangerous this is.

The voices dissolve into nothing.

I want to ask Jim if he thinks we can do this, but I think he's leaning on me to lead here.

"This might be the toughest thing I've ever done," he says.

His words float and infect everything around us. I can't let it go unanswered.

"I know," I say. "Somethings need to be done."

"If there is a God, this is surely a sin," he says.

"I thought you didn't believe that," I say. "And it's not a sin," I say, hoping to squash that thought. But Jim's right. Talking out there in the desert was easy enough. Doing it here seems much harder. It's as if the air in the compound, exhaled by everyone here, all of John's supporters, is poisoned. I feel weak just thinking about what we're plotting.

"If you say so," Jim says.

"Listen," I say and grab his elbow. "You have to be with this one hundred percent."

"I am," he says, though his tone seems to be ambivalent.

"We're *going* to get this done," I say.

He nods. Not the attitude I want, but I don't have much of a choice.

More voices splash outside the walls. This time they're in prayer. For a moment I close my eyes, feeling a oneness to people I don't know.

"You know Skinner's pigeons?" Jim asks.

"I've heard," I say, not wanting to get into an argument about religion. "What does that have to do with anything?" We don't need to waste time thinking philosophical things. We need to get started. Before the guillotine drops. John might be out there, his eyes and ears zooming in on us.

"That's all we are, you know that?" he says.

"Really?" I say, not wanting this argument; one that reminds me too much of MacGee.

"Everything in this world is random. Especially the horrible things. Always at random. We react in stupid ways. Sometimes it's a hymn, sometimes it's trying to kill others for no reason."

This is not helping. Is he talking about us? Is he trying to backtrack?

"Life is always random," I say, hoping that will shut him up.

He raises a hand to stop me from saying anything else. His eyes are on the table, as if he's thinking really hard about this. Are these the last words of a man walking to his death?

"That's what that," he jerks his head at the prayer, "is. It's pigeons pecking. And it's worth jack-all. So is trying to kill for no reason"

"But we're not pigeons," I reply. "For us, it's not rituals, it's ideas that go hand in hand with them." I'm wary about getting into an argument, but I won't let his pessimism stand. I know where that can lead. The deaths of two friends have shown me that.

"The ideas are just a cover up we tell to make ourselves feel smart. It's when the randomness becomes nothing but bad luck, a streak unlike we have ever seen that the ideas become nothing. Dust. And we'll see ourselves for the pigeons that we are."

I jump at footsteps outside my door. At any moment John's men could come bursting in here, and we'll have nothing to defend ourselves with. And Jim wants to argue about some stupid theory of his.

"And so what?" I say, my voice low and gruff. "What if they are stupid ideas? You either have ideas or you have nothing. And when the time comes, it's better to have ideas that have been tested in tough times," I say, spittle flying out of my mouth. "Because ideas, like the ones before the fall, will end up being worthless, and you might as well have an idea that has stood the test of time." I surprise myself with my vehemence. My fists are clenched, and I'm mentally daring Jim to come up with more.

Jim looks at me like he's disappointed.

"Listen, we're trying to build for the future, right?" I ask, not knowing where I'm going with this. MacGee's words, nothing exact, just his timbre, floats in the back of my head. I'm doing this for him. This will be laid at his altar. And it will be laid at Jenny's altar. And in the end I will be clean. I will be vindicated.

"Is that what it is?" Jim asks.

"It is. And the idea we had in the desert still applies. For Mitt, for Craig. We're doing this for peace."

Jim doesn't nod, but he doesn't disagree.

I wait until the silence freezes into awkwardness between us. This isn't how two men on a mission are supposed to part, but I don't have the patience for much more.

I bid Jim goodbye and walk to my room to find my handgun. Genevine and Rusty step out.

"What is it?" Genevine asks.

There's nothing in my room. Where did I last see my handgun? Someone must have taken it. My pulse picks up, my skin warms. John's more cunning than I ever thought. My throat tightens. I will lose. The thought echoes in my head. I feel under my pillow. Nothing. I throw it, and sit down on the floor. My eye catches something underneath the bed. A box. I pull it out. It's an old cigar box. I look up at Genevine. She nods. Inside the box is a revolver. My heart jumps, then I look at Genevine.

"May I?" I ask.

"Of course," she says. Rusty is behind her, tugging at her dress.

I check for ammunition and find the gun empty. I look around, gasping for air, it's like a noose is around my neck. "You see any bullets?" I ask.

"I have more guns," Genevine says. "A 1911, though I'm sure you don't know anything about that."

"You do?" I ask.

"And you have a .38," she says. Underneath our bed she pulls out more boxes. She opens one. In her hand there's now a gun that looks bigger than her head. "No one knows about these," she says, batting Rusty's hand as the girl reaches for a box. "Not yet sweetie, you'll learn soon enough."

I stare at my gun. Genevine hands me a box with bullets. "That should help," she says.

"Thanks," I say. "No one knows about these?" I ask.

"Of course not," she says.

I look over at Rusty. "You can't say anything about this to anyone."

Rusty nods.

Trying to measure the weight of the air, to see how much I should trust either of them, I stroke the gun in my hand. The cold metal comforts me. I load it with bullets. Each one clicking in when it nestles into it's resting place. Funny thing, to look at a bullet and know that this can kill a man.

"You'll need this too," Genevine says and pulls out a long knife from a box. "It was my father's."

I don't know much about this woman I claim to love. "Thank you," I say, a sting hits my eyes, and I fight back tears.

"So what are you up to?" she asks.

I can smell her sour sweat from here. The blood in my body streams around my body faster and faster. I want her. I love her. But if that's the case, should I tell her what I'm doing?

She rolls her eyes. "You still don't want to tell me anything, do you? I thought you were done with lying to me."

"I am," I say.

We both take a look at Rusty.

"You want me to leave?" the girl asks.

"Don't," I say.

"Then tell us," Rusty replies.

"I'm thinking… I'm not lying," I say. "But there needs to be a change…" Do I actually say this to them? I might be risking everything. "At the compound. With the flock."

"Whatever do you mean?" Genevine asks; her head tilts slightly.

"I know what he means," Rusty says, a grin on her beaming face.

I don't reply.

"And you mind telling me what that is?" Genevine asks me.

"We want peace, don't we?" I ask.

"Even the hero?" Her voice's laced with sarcasm.

"Yes, even a hero understands what's needed for peace."

"And you're going to convince all these men that we need peace?" she asks.

"That's right," I say.

"How?" she asks. Her face is tinged with pride and pity.

"I'll need your help," I say and point to the gun. "You'll have to help me. Watch my back incase people are plotting against me." I give Rusty a nod.

"What are you planning?" Genevine asks.

"I don't know," I blurt out.

"You don't know? I think you'd better be sure you know."

"It's hard to explain," I say as I get up. "And I know I don't have much leeway with you after the stunt I pulled. But if I'm to succeed, I'll need your help." And as I say this, it strikes me as true. I don't have many allies, and I need to get eyes to counter the people John has.

"You have my help," Rusty says. She's smiling, looking for a pat on the head. I give it to her, though I'd rather have the feisty-eyed girl I first knew.

"Leave us for a second, Rusty. Please?" Genevine asks. Her tone already sharp.

Rusty winks at me and runs out of the room.

"You don't even think about the consequences of your actions, do you?" Genevine asks when the door shuts.

"I do."

"What?"

"I… Know what happens if I don't do this."

"Oh, you do?" Genevine steps up to me.

There's not much for me to go on, but I square off with her. She has the .45 in hand. "There'll be no rest for any of us."

"And did you stop once to think about us?"

"I asked you to help—"

"I meant once you get crushed, because John's been crushing the likes of you for ages. Since he was a teen he knew how to outwit men twice his age. You'll be nothing to him. And so will we."

She must have heard some of our conversation. Part of me wonders if she'll run out of here and tell others what I'm planning. "All the more reason for you to help me," I say.

The slap shakes me out of my cocoon, and my cheek warms up from her hand.

"How dare you put me in this position," Genevine says.

Her words sting harder than her hand. I search for something to say.

"How dare you put her in this position," she says, pointing at the door.

"I… I know this sounds hard, but it has to be done."

"Why?"

"John will lead us all to our deaths."

"How? He may be a bastard, but he's led us so far."

"And he got lucky," I say, hoping to keep my true emotions out of this. "He's going to bring us a wrath like you won't believe. And I won't have it," I say.

"You won't? John took you in, and treated you like a brother. This is how you repay him?"

That cuts me. I've never heard her speak of John in this manner. "It's more than just me."

"It's MacGee. The man *you* killed," she says, her finger jutting out at me.

With all my might I make sure not to reach out and grab that finger. "It's not him."

"It is," she says with too much confidence. "You want to blame John for all this."

"We need peace if we are to survive," I say. "John won't let that be." When I see that her face doesn't crack, that she's staring at me with an intense hatred that's too close to what Jenny once used on me, I think for another tactic. "You haven't seen the violence that he's caused."

"And were you that much better?" she asks. "You've survived this long by being peaceful?"

She's smart, Genevine.

"You're pointing a finger at me?" I ask, somewhat angry. "Do you even know what I've done?"

"I can smell it off you. I saw it in bed. Your eyes, are always looking elsewhere. You've killed women, haven't you?" Her finger is in my face. I grab it and jerk it away. I hear a pop.

"Don't you dare act like you know what I've been through," I say through a clenched jaw. Her face doesn't back down, and I remember that she has a gun in her other hand.

"What do you think would have happened to Rusty if I wasn't here? Or if John had his way?" I say and let go of her finger. "Think for a goddamn second. You think she'd be free in any house? John was willing to let the other soldiers have her as they please."

Her face softens, her eyes cast down to her feet.

"No answer?" I continue. "No smart ass reply? Because you do know what I'm talking about, don't you?" I step up so I can whisper it in her ear. She seems hurt, and it might be wise to stop, but I can't.

"They would have run a train on her. Each man. Maybe twenty of them would have raped her to death. You get that, don't you? Your mighty John would have let that be. So go on and tell Rusty that you don't give a fuck about her."

Silence. Her eyes are still on the floor, motionless.

A part of me wants to be quiet, soothe her.

"Do you want me to tell her? Or are you going to help me?" I ask.

After a few moments, and what seems to be a lifetime, I walk to the door to open it up.

"All right," she says.

"What?"

"You're right. I'll help."

We embrace and kiss. I feel her body press up on mine.

"Thank you," I say. "I know it's hard, but we'll get it done."

She nods. We kiss again. I taste her salty mouth.

Rusty knocks on the door. "Can I come in?" she asks.

Genevine's cheeks are flushed. There's nothing in this world I would like more than to make love to her, but there's work to be done.

Rusty comes in. She's uncomfortable in our unconsummated silence.

"You know what you have to do?" I ask Genevine.

She nods.

"Do it. Teach her how to at least handle a gun. She deserves to be able to protect herself," I say.

Rusty's eyes gleam.

"Okay," Genevine says.

"I'll be back." Is there anything else I can tell them? "If John's minions ask about me, just say you had a fight with me and don't care for me."

"I will."

I put tuck the gun into my belt, and stuff the knife on the other side. The blade, though sheathed, digs into my skin, but I ignore it. I leave.

Outside the clouds don't seem like the high dome that they usually are. Today they seem low and pregnant. The air, though chilly, is humid. Everyone is louder than normal, bustling around. Something's different. I head to where I think Samantha will be. I see her with a flock of women around her. They're talking, excited. I walk past them, and I feel the slice of her eyes on me. My body remembers those nights where her gasp was only for me, and I walk even faster trying to make sure that my arousal isn't there for everyone to see.

A group of guards walk past me. I'm sure I recognize a few of them from the night MacGee died. They flash me looks of hunters, like they're supposed to take me down next. I smile and wave. "A blessed day, brothers," I say.

They act confused, and a few of them wave back, their faces still solemn.

I sniff the air and the aroma of moist soil overwhelms me. Is it going to rain? Surely my senses are playing games with me.

I see Jim, surrounded by a few men. He flinches when he sees me, then beckons me over. I finger the gun in my belt just to make sure it's there.

"How's it going?" I ask as I step into the circle. The other men, four of them, look familiar. Their eyes are all downcast, and they don't look at me for more than a few seconds. It's as if they've been caught in the act.

"Good," Jim says, giving me a firm embrace. "Tom, fellas. Excuse us for a moment." He takes me aside.

"They good?" I ask.

"They're solid. They're behind you all the way. All of them are team leaders of some sort. They can probably get at least a few guys apiece."

"They look familiar," I say.

"All soldiers. Hard as rocks. We can trust them."

I stare and realize that I recognize at least one face.

"What's wrong?" Jim asks.

"I think I recognize some of them from the cave. The one where they had some of us held as hostages."

"I know," Jim says. "They said they remember you coming in and helping them. That's the main reason they're on your side. Why?"

My instincts tell me that these men are bad, that the story Thomas told me about them was true, and that they are nothing more than rapists.

"No reason. If you say they're tough and good to go, then I'll take your word for it," I say. A young couple walks by us, and we exchange greetings. I watch them disappear around a corner. The air is heavy. John's people could be anywhere. I need anyone I can get. "What have you told them?"

"We need to stick together no matter... I left the real matter for later."

"Nothing about John then?"

"No."

We head back over to talk to them.

"How's it going gentlemen?" I say as I shake their hands.

"Good," they reply. No one seems nervous.

"I'm Tom."

They just nod their heads. They're smart enough not to want their names out in the open. Not sure what to make of this, I decide not to make a huge deal. Jim knows them.

"From now on we will work in secrecy. You have it from the highest power that we're under attack, right?" I say.

They all nod.

"And to fight this attack we must root out the evil amongst us. They may claim to work on the side of God, but that's what the devil has always done. We don't know who that is, but we will work tirelessly to figure that out," I say and hear a round of yeses. Jim is rocking his head.

"Well, this is how it's going to be. You'll work for me. But in the end we're doing this for the good of everyone here. Understood?" I say.

They agree in nods.

"You might not hear from me, but Jim'll give you little pieces of information and you will execute. Got it?"

"Yes," they say, some energy in their voices.

I embrace them all and take Jim aside again. His face is nervous as well.

"You figure out who hates me. Pretend you hate me for that matter. And we'll see what we can do about them," I say.

"And them?"

"Tell them to look around and be eyes and ears for you. No talking about me, but meet with them every hour, it will to keep them in touch."

"I don't think it's a good idea letting them go out of sight," Jim says.

"Why not?"

He grinds his teeth, the lines of his jaw appearing and disappearing.

"What are you going to do with John's men? I'm sure there are more of them than us," he asks.

"Not together, though. We'll figure a way to separate them."

"That's your plan, isn't it? You think this will be easy?" Jim asks.

"Are you backing out?" I ask.

"I'm not. I want to make sure that you have a plan at least."

"I do. Just hold up your end. And remember what this is for."

That seems to toughen him up.

"You seen John around?" I ask.

"Not today."

"I'll find out where he is."

"And...?"

"Just do your part. I'll meet you in front of my place before lunch," I say as I walk away.

I turn past a corner and hear a psst sound. Between two houses, a figure stands. Did they hear us talking?

"Hi there," the voice says, soft.

My blood runs down to my groin. It's her.

"Hi Samantha." I look behind me. There's no one around. Don't do anything stupid. You need to be sharp. And you can't do anything that will cut you down in standing. Don't fall for lust, I tell myself over and over.

"Tom, you've been avoiding me," she says patting my thigh.

I swallow, use all my might to fight back the desire that's erupting from my heart. My senses are clear and the curves of her body are highlighted. The monster inside me is creeping out again. The one that appeared that night with Jenny. No. Not now. You're going to clean yourself. Don't do this, or think of pushing inside Samantha.

"I've been busy," I say, controlling my voice, though it's dipped into something extremely low.

"You're girlfriend's very jealous," she says.

"Wife."

"She's so mean. And all I want to do is drop off some food. Is that so bad?"

Taking deep breaths, I wonder how I can change the subject. She has strings to my lust, and she knows exactly how to pull them. "Who were all those women you were talking to?" I ask.

"Oh, don't worry, we just talk about you." She smiles.

"They listen to you?" I ask.

"Of course. They love me. I'm the only woman who dares to speak her mind."

We stop as some men walk by us on the main throughway. They don't notice us.

Samantha leans in; her warm hands touch my cock, her lips brush against my cheek.

"I'm pregnant... It's yours," she says, and leans back from me, her eyes flirtatious.

That knocks the air out of me. "A-Are you sure?"

"Don't worry. James thinks it's his," she says.

Focus, I need to focus on the task at hand. "Very well," I say, my throat dry. "I'm going to need your help. You need to spread the good word about me."

"I do?"

I hesitate. Is her voice enticing me, or mocking me? "Please," I say. "I need your help."

"Oh," she says, her voice drops a note and she's serious, again. The change is bothersome, but I force myself to ignore it.

"Can you—"

"Everyone already thinks highly of you," she says. "I can say more, but you're already a hero. You know that?"

"I do. But things might get rough soon. Put in a good word, even if my name heads for the worse, all right?"

"You're John's right-hand man, what could possibly go wrong?" she asks.

"Can you do that much?"

She smiles. "You're up to no good, Tom. But I like it. I will."

"I'll see you around?" I say.

"Soon," she says.

As I walk away from Samantha, needles ripple across my skin. Is it from her, or is it something else? I touch my gun. Then the handle of my knife. I'll never be taken alive.

No one on the street seems to recognize me. Something's wrong. I decide to head over and talk to John. The mere thought sends spasms to my heart, and I walk faster. Staring at the ground, for some reason concerned about tripping, my mind transports me to the first night with Jenny, as well as when I thought I'd found a friend in MacGee. I round a corner and come up on the torture building. There's a guard outside. A tall lanky man, with a head of an axed pumpkin. He follows me with one eye—the other one stares straight ahead.

"Hi," I say, meandering up to him.

He scowls, deep lines appearing out of nowhere on his young face.

"No one's allowed in there."

I can see that it's locked from the outside. My mind, a loose animal right now, gallops to the idea that inside could be Jim or one of the other men I just talked to. I step closer to the door and don't hear anything.

"No one here?" I ask.

He shakes his head then jerks it still, another scowl appearing on his face. "Not to know."

His speaks like his vocal chord is in his chest, allowing for the throat to slur them.

"It's fine, do you know me?" I ask.

"No."

"You should. I'm with John. His best friend. I'm the one who just came from the desert," I say. "I've seen the Light of God, so don't mess with me."

That seems to slap some sense into him. "You're with John," he finally says.

"Of course. Did he put you up to this?"

"All I know is that I am the guard."

"And no one can go in there?" I say.

He nods his head, long harsh nods. His neck creaks at each direction change.

"Well, they gave you the key at least?"

"They did." He reaches inside the top of his shirt and pulls out a key tied around his neck. It shines, and he stares at it, his mouth open.

"Well, good job."

With all his attention on the key, I look over at the door. Does the body remember a place of personal tragedy? The chills in my gut say yes. This is where MacGee died. Where Thomas realized that his betrayal was final. I hate this place. It's evil, and it makes those who enter it evil too. Then something hits me. I can use it.

"I'll tell you something… What was your name?"

The man stuffs his key down his shirt greedily, and eyes me. "I'm Harkin."

"Well, Harkin, I'll let you know what this place is going to be used for. But you have to promise not to tell anyone, all right?"

"Okay…" he says, breathing faster.

"Well. There are some bad men here. In this compound and we're going to have to get them in there. You're going to help me do that, all right?"

He jerks his head into a nod.

"I want you to leave—"

"I'm the guard," he says, suddenly angry.

"That's right. You are. And you're no doorman. Only doormen stand in front of doors. I want you to guard."

I wait for that to sink in. It might be too much for him.

"Okay," he says.

"I want you to go where the vehicles are and find me some gasoline. You know where they keep it?"

More nods.

"Well, find it and bring a couple gallons to that house there," I say, pointing in the direction of my house. "It's the one with blue paint on the door."

"Okay. Then I come back here?"

"No, wait there. I'll find you. If anyone asks, tell them it's being done for John." I think about any other items I may be forgetting. Before I can say anything, he's bounded away, his mouth open, and his eyes bright.

I head over to my house. My hope is that Harkin has the only key and that if he stays away from the torture building, I can delay whatever it is John has planned.

Rusty is inside.

"What are you up to?" I ask. She pulls out a revolver, it's small, but she points it at me. For a second all my plans are flushed from my mind as I remember that Rusty, the nice girl, has every reason to kill me.

"Rusty," I say slowly, "what are you doing?"

She smiles and points the gun at the wall next to me and pulls the trigger. The hammer drops.

"I'm practicing. Genevine showed me how to use one. She said I should practice with it before I shoot people." She pulls out a handful of bullets.

It comes out of her mouth so innocently that my mind takes a few seconds before it realizes what's before me. "She home?" I ask, breathing deeply, trying to ignore the image of the sweet girl and her gun. After all, she *does* need to know how to shoot. If I fail, it may be the only thing that will save her, or at least give some of the men some pause before they rape her.

"She's gone."

I explain to Rusty that she needs to keep the door locked and that only one man, with a key around his neck, should be allowed inside. She agrees. Her eyes still don't reflect any hate. I turn to leave.

"Where are you going?" she asks.

I still have to see John. He's hatching something, which means I need to find out what, and barring that, I need to be right by him.

"I'm going to help some people," I say.

"No you're not," she says, the sweetness drained from her voice. Now it's a mix of adulthood and fear.

"What makes you say that?"

"You're not helping anyone but yourself."

"Genevine tell you that?"

"No. But I'm not dumb," she says. "You know the caves you found me in?"

I'd rather not talk about this, rather not have her form better memories of me killing her loved ones, yet I have to at least nod.

"Well. That wasn't my home."

"No?"

"No, it was a place I found afterwards."

"After the fall?"

"That's right. I'm from Seattle."

"You came all the way from Seattle to here?" I ask.

"I was hiking with my family. We were doing a family trip. The last one before my mom and dad were going to get divorced."

I take her hand so she can go on.

"We were in a gully when it happened. The skies turned to sun, then to coal. My mother watched it from higher ground. She went blind." She holds out her hands into fists. "Burned out her retinas."

I imagine someone stumbling blindly.

"We started to walk to find a hospital. But that was foolish."

"Nothing but ashes?" I ask, knowing what I saw.

"Not everywhere. It wasn't the ashes, but the people who realized that we were truly alone. Everyone was alone. I think it took a couple days to settle in and some people were helping others when the bad ones came for us all."

She says the ones like it's a fatal disease.

"They got my mother when she had gone off for water. My dad couldn't do anything as a gang of men took turns on her. We didn't have a gun, only a knife."

Though Rusty's staring at me, she's not looking at me. Her voice is monotone, and without emotion. It's frightening to think that she's just a child.

"He was trembling. My dad, and whenever I asked why we weren't doing anything, he just told me to be quiet. We walked off and he never looked back. That night the same men came for us. I woke up to see my mother's head in the fire. My dad didn't stand a chance. I slipped out of one man's grip and ran. They didn't chase me. I watched from high ground. Then what they did to my mother, they did to him. Over and over."

I want to hug her. "I'm sorry," I say, not knowing what else to say. I crouch next to her.

She glances at me, a pitying look in her eye. "I'm fine. I walked back to camp later that night. I knew which one was the leader. I looked into his eyes when I woke him up and told him I wanted him, and only him."

Now I really want to ask how old she is. Surely this couldn't have been the only way she could have survived? And yet a voice speaks up, reminding me that I wasn't so pure myself. What choice did I leave Jenny?

"What did he do?" I ask.

"He took me in."

Do I ask what that means? Her voice sounds like an old woman's. I feel fear run through me.

"Then one night, after I had learned how to please him, please him until disgusting things came out, and he smelled of sweet sweat…"

Now I see emotion, pure hatred like never before. This could be something reserved for me.

"I let them all sleep, pulled out his grenade, and ran… All of them were mangled and dead. I came back for their guns. I never felt happier in my life. I found the caves you saw me in a few weeks later. I thought they were nice people at first."

"Did they hurt you?" I ask.

"They were better than most," she says. "But I wish I was happy as I was that night. I also wish that I didn't stop hating my dad."

My fault, I'm thinking, it's all my fault, though I'm not sure why this thought keeps going through my head.

She reaches and touches my face. I half hope to feel better, but instead I feel sick. Is it because of knowing what she had to do to survive? If that's the case, then *I* should revolt everyone.

"You—" she tries to speak.

"Well, I don't know how much better I am," I say through an emotionally constricted throat. "I've done a lot of evil to be where I am today."

"So have I," she says.

What child should ever have to say that?

"I've done worse," I say. This time a current passes through me that tells me it's foolish to confess to a child. What can I possibly gain?

"That doesn't matter. You're going to get them, right?" she asks.

"I…"

"Then tell me how I can help," she says, that violence, hatred, dripping off her face.

It takes a moment for me to recover from that sense that this girl is evil and there's no going back, and that, furthermore, I might be worse than her.

"Do as I say and stay here, wait for that man," I say.

She nods, taking my face in her hands. "It has to be done."

And I want to cry, weep in her hands, me a man. "Thank you," I say standing up, straightening my posture.

I feel her eyes on my back, as I leave.

Around John's front door are several guards. They're speaking in hushed voices. The air is damp, and turning more electrified. Is it the fear that today might be my last day?

"Hi Tom," one of the men says, as the three other guards step away from him to face me. My hairs stand on end, and I picture shooting them all down.

"What's going on?" I ask.

"Nothing," the man says and looks at his friends. The man has a black birthmark on his forehead shaped like an explosion. "Why, something going on with you?"

The way he emphasizes "you" pushes me away from civility.

"Nothing at all," I say. All of them have rifles over their shoulders, but they aren't moving for them. So I try to control the pressure on my head, the one pushing me towards shooting them all down. "Is John here?"

"He's inside with a council member," the man says.

"When will he be out? I need to talk to him right away."

"He'll be out soon."

"Knock," I say.

The man doesn't expect that, and he hesitates, then turns his head to look at his friends.

"I didn't say talk to your girlfriends, I said to knock," I say.

He nods, shrinking in size, and knocks on the door.

"What is it?" John's voice asks, vibrating across the thick door.

"It's Tom, sir."

A pause. Murmurs. "Let him in."

The door opens, and I step inside. John is standing next to a short bald man with loose jowls.

"Tom," the council member says and embraces me. "So good to see our hero."

It's fake, this man's voice, and I glance uncomfortably at John. Perhaps I'm out of my element here. There's that frigid silence that tells me I might be in trouble.

"We were just talking about you," John says.

"I hope I wasn't disturbing something important," I say as I embrace John.

"Oh, no. You were expected," the council member says.

"For what?" I ask. If they can predict my movements like this, what hope do I have to get this job done?

"Nothing big," the councilman says.

John's eyes parse me. "Just the discussion of your travels."

He must be concerned about the Light of God. Jim was right. I fight the itch to reach for my gun. "The retaliation must be swift," I say. "We cannot hesitate."

"That's right," John replies. His eyes flitter around mine. He doesn't trust me.

I try to keep my brain from screaming. If this is it, let it come. But my knees are shaking. Am I that scared again? Did I not vanquish every man who has so far challenged me? Try to think of MaGee, I say to myself, try to think of Rusty.

Without warning my body speaks to my brain. That feeling outside. The air, the electricity. I've felt it before.

"It's going to rain," I blurt out.

"Rain?" says the council member; his face wrinkles up like a bag. "That hasn't happened since The Fall. It's not going to rain. It's been like this before."

"We should get ready," I say, a little less certain. "Save some of the water in a reservoir. Or at least celebrate."

"Did God tell you this?" the council member asks.

"Are you challenging me?" To John I say: "You believe me, don't you?"

"If it's true, we'll have to get ready," John says. His mouth moves after he's done speaking. I'm sure he doesn't believe me.

"Leave us," John says, his voice turning into a boom.

"Something's off about him," I say as soon as the man closes the door.

"Is that right?" John says, his tone mocking. "Why's that, Tom?"

My name flies off his tongue with spittle.

"His style. You trust him?" I ask, grabbing John's eyes with mine and trying to bring him closer.

John blinks. "I have no reason not to. What did you hear?"

I feel the tingling turn into something other than fear. Now I know my fate. Not the result, but what I will do, what my DNA will do until I'm dirt. Rusty knew it when she spoke to me. So did Jenny. As well as MacGee. There's nothing I can do but accept it.

"Nothing, but I can sniff it on him. Beware," I say, still grabbing his eyes with mine. "For example I knew that I could trust you from the moment I saw you. I knew you were one with God." I'm sucking John's strength.

John nods, but he takes the movement to release his eyes from me, and he seems to regain his composure. "As I felt for you, Tom."

This time my name sounds respected on his tongue.

"Thank you," I say, trying to look, and thus feel, moved by his words. "We will only bring The Kingdom if we stick together."

John's still not believing everything I'm saying. "You're right," he says.

I take a moment to look at the map. I hope that out there Jim is doing his part. If he was to turn weak on me... I don't even want to think. Just do what you were meant to do. Be yourself.

"You really think it will rain?" he asks.

"I feel it."

"All right, then we'd better get everyone ready. You know what time?"

"Not certain. Just that it will today or tonight."

He smiles. "Just like a weatherman. Never any certainties, right?"

I smile, even though I don't know if he's mocking me, or making a friendly joke. "That's right."

I let that hang in the air, hoping it stirs up some good feelings in him. My strength is leaving, but I know what needs to be done, and that's even more important.

"You know the story of the original Fall, Tom?" John asks.

"Of course, who doesn't?" I say.

"You know how Lucifer was kicked out because he thought he could challenge God?"

"He chose to rule in Hell rather than serve in Heaven," I say, trepidation building inside me.

"Well, he was punished for it in the end. But he continuously tries to bring us down when he whispers in our ears, trying to make us like him."

I'm not sure where he's going with this. "Well then, I'm glad we know how to defeat him," I say.

"We do. Or we think we do. You know Judas? He was talked to by Lucifer, and he fell into his trap."

"Indeed he did," I say.

"And we have to stop that," John says.

173

"Of course, otherwise how do we bring about the Lord's Kingdom?" I say, hoping that he believes me. "Who do you suspect?" I ask. "Anyone in the council?"

John's face is still unmovable. "We're not certain, but we're looking."

"What makes you think it?"

"We've had some people come up to us as say so."

I cock my head, acting confused. "Surely there's more than a little hearsay?"

"We have to always be vigilant."

"That's a shame," I say, shaking my head. "And just when our external enemies are getting ready to fight us."

"That's how it always happens," John says. He seems more sure of me now.

"We have to be careful," I say.

"It's one of the soldiers."

I let out the start of a laugh. "A soldier?" I shake my head. "Were they at either of the recent battles?"

"That's what I'm hearing."

"And what about the people who came up to you with this info?" I ask.

"What do you mean?"

"They people you trust? Because it might just be a personal thing, or them playing us." I hold John's stare.

"I didn't think of that," John says. "You're right, we should be wary of that."

"We should. I'll tell everyone I know to keep an eye out."

John pauses for a second. "Tell them to be careful."

"I will."

And cries sound out from outside. At first it's a few punctuating the air. Then it comes out as a chorus. I run out, John behind me.

The sky is much like the morning, though darker. But I smell rain melted with old dust-ridden sand. I take in a deep breath. A drop of rain hits my head. I smile at John. He returns the favor. There's no more stress on his face.

"You were right," he says.

I suppress the urge to say of course. "It's gift from the Lord to us. Let's get everyone ready."

We head over to where a group of soldiers are standing and staring at the sky.

"Everyone," John yells. "Get every vessel that can hold liquid out in the open."

We run and help cover some motors, as well as pull other vehicles into the open. Funny how you can get so used to one kind of weather, that when it changes it's almost like magic.

"Do we have seeds?" I ask.

"Good point," John says.

My mind is thinking about how else to use this rain, when the patters turn into a waterfall. I'm drenched in no time. There's a cry of relief, almost a moan, that rises above the rain. And a flash lights up the shadows of the cloud. The crack and boom shakes my skin, and brings a warmth to my belly.

John stands next to me, his arm on my shoulder. "I talked to the engineers," he says. "They were ready for such a contingency. A reservoir is being filled as we speak."

"That's great. We'll be better off. Are there seeds to plant?" I ask.

"They're getting to it."

I pat John on his shoulder. I'm soaked, cold, but I don't want to leave the rain. The rain stings my skin, and I hope to remember this.

We stand there, watching children run about in the small streams, splashing and ignoring their parents' pleas.

"We're going to be fine," I say, as the rain softens.

"You're right," John says. "Look."

I follow his finger to the horizon. There's a shaft of light a few miles away. It's tearing through the cloud cover and lighting up a hill. As if God Himself's reaching down with a finger.

I remember the moment I had seen a ray of light highlighting a plant. That day I'd that mother as hostage, after I had taken her family hostage. How I felt so full of hope. How she didn't reply to my observation, and how she tried to kill me, even though I'd spared her. And now John is telling me the same thing. What does that make him? I smile.

Images of MacGee and Jenny and Rusty pass through my head. I remember the day that I kissed John's hand. I tremble, anger passing through my body.

"That looks like a sign from God," I say.

He nods his head, eyes on the shafts of light. I know what it's there for.

The rain has slowed to a drizzle. The earth smells clean. Why wouldn't someone believe in a new beginning? But what does it matter what someone believes? I know what really matters.

"I'm going to look around," I say. "I want to make sure that there's no one hatching anything. You keep an eye out as well," I say.

"Godspeed," John says.

I pause. I don't need John snooping around, either. "I'll meet you back in your place in a half an hour," I say.

John nods, his eyes on the shafts of light.

At my house, I see no one outside. I assume that Harkin's either inside or playing in the rain. In front of the torture house there's no one as well. All the better. I find Jim, near where I last saw him.

"You find any more?" I ask, taking him by the arm and leading him into an alley.

"I found a few more," he says.

"Who's against us?"

"I found a lot of those," he said. "The young assholes patrolling the streets are all for John."

"He suspects something. Anyone ask you questions?"

Jim shakes his head.

"We need to move now. Get the people on our side together," I say.

"They are."

"Do you think they'll kill for us?" I ask.

Jim pauses. That means no.

"None that might stand by at least?"

"Maybe," Jim says.

"Maybe? Do you understand what happens with maybe? We die."

"What's your plan?" he asks.

"We take a group of John's men to the torture house. We'll lock them in there. Telling them to wait, it's an ambush for traitors."

These words, the inkling of a plan I'm making up as I go seem to lend some spirits to Jim's eyes. "Then what?"

"I'll deal with that part. But we'll be able to weaken him."

"It'll take more than a few lost men to weaken John. Some people are claiming that he brought the rain here."

"What?" I say then jerk my head, and clench my fist. "Where are our men?"

"They're doing what you told them to."

I need to act. Whatever good will I have with John won't last longer than the rain. "Get a handful of John's men. Explain to them that they need to lay in ambush in the torture house for an enemy of John."

"What are you going to do?"

"I'll meet you in the front. I'll unlock it."

"Why don't you come with me?" he asks, his face nervous.

"Christ, let's go."

Running, my feet splash through puddles, and over kids rolling in mud. My mind's tense, wondering what I'll say to these people when I see them. And what will happen when they don't listen to me.

"There," Jim points.

It's a group of men, all young. One might be the kid I showed up many nights ago. They all scowl at me when I land in a puddle and soak half of them.

"You heard the news?" I ask, gasping for air next to them.

They look at each other. There's something in their movements that tells me they don't trust me.

I snap my fingers. "Dammit, answer me."

"No," one short, loose-skinned one says.

"John didn't say anything about a mole in our midst? An agent of Lucifer?"

"Well…" the man says.

"We have to set up a trap for him, quickly." I look over at Jim who nods. He's at least got the common sense to imitate my movements, and act like time is ticking down.

"Where—"

"No time. You the brave guys, right?" I ask.

The men nod in unison this time.

"Well we need you to wait in the interrogation room," I say. "We'll bring him in later, but it has to be a surprise. You have knives?" I ask.

Some nod.

"Good. Let's get this show on the road."

They seem hesitant. I glance around, making sure that John doesn't sneak up on me.

"Let's go, men. Time's a wasting," Jim says. His voice has taken that militaristic tone again. The men fall in line. Jim and I run in front.

"I'll break off for the key. You take them to the front," I say and head off to my place.

Inside, Harkin is braiding Rusty's hair.

"Hi there," I say, but he's too mesmerized to say anything to me. He stares at her hair as he strokes it and overlaps one strand over another.

"Hi Tom," Rusty says, waving at me with her gun in her hand. "I found a new friend," she says and winks at me.

"She's my friend," Harkin says, a grin spreads to half his face.

I walk over and kiss her. "Glad you've found a friend. Harkin is a good man."

"I am," Harkin says. "And Rusty is a good girl."

"That's right," I say. "You get the fuel, like I said?"

"Harkin got all the fuel," he says and points with one hand at two barrels next to the door. They're tied together with one large pipe. He must be strong.

"Harkin, I need the key," I say placing my hand palm up.

Harkin stops what he's doing and looks up. "Harkin is the guard."

"I know Harkin. But right now I need the key. Your job as a guard is over. You now have a new job," I say. I feel Rusty place her hand on me. I shut up.

"Harkin, forget about the key," Rusty says. "Let's play here."

Harkin seems confused.

"You can keep the key Harkin," I say. "But then playtime is over, and there won't be any way for you to find out the next secret job."

"A secret job?" Rusty asks, her eyes widen, and glint with the knowledge of her act.

"That's right," I say.

"For me?" Harkin asks.

"For you. But if you don't want it, that's fine," I say.

"Can I?" Rusty asks.

"Sure—"

"NO. Harkin's job is secret," Harkin says, standing up.

I hold out my hand, and he places the key in it.

"Thank you. Now come here," I say. "In ten minutes. No more, no less. I want you to go outside and pour the gasoline all over the building you were guarding. Then I want you to light it on fire."

Harkin nods like he's wanted this job his entire life.

"And there will be people trying to stop you, but you go on and do it. Know that you're doing the work of God."

"I am," Harkin says, proud.

"And the devil inside might try to break out, but you don't listen to what he says. Got it?"

Harkin nods.

I look over at Rusty. "Make sure it's in ten minutes that he's over there."

Rusty nods, then points her finger at her chest. I point my finger at Harkin. She nods.

I head outside, the rain has died down and people seem to be going about like normal. I see Jim and the men in front of the building.

"So tell me what we're doing here again?" asks one of the men. His nose and jaw seem to be replicas of each other.

"Ambush," I say as I open the door. No one seems to be paying attention. "Unless you're chicken, and don't care for the Lord's work."

The men stay silent.

"Stay in here and don't so much as whisper. John and I will bring the bastard over. Then when the door opens, you get him."

They file in. I can't believe they're doing so, and I suppress a smile. I lock the door behind him.

Behind Jim I see a head dart from around a corner. It takes a second for my brain to realize it was the council member I saw with John earlier today. Did he hear what I had to say?

"What?" Jim asks as I brush by him.

"Stop him," I hiss. There are people milling about, so I don't take off running right away. I head to a parallel street and walk as fast as I can. Jim has the sense to head down another alley. A few kids splash in a muddy pool. They're dark, except for their smiles. One splashes me as I jump over them.

I need to find this council member before he finds John. I bump into him on the next corner. He turns as he was looking behind him.

"Oh. Oh," he says.

I grab him by his neck. One of the kids peeks his head around the corner.

"Are you gonna fight him?" the kid asks asks.

"No, go away," I say. My other hand hovers above my knife handle. The man struggles to break my grip. The kid leaves and I drag the man between two buildings. Jim appears.

"He hear us?" Jim asks.

"Did you?" I ask, pulling out my knife and holding it to his neck.

"No questions," Jim asks. "He did, or he didn't. And right now he did." He turns to see if anyone else will come around the corner.

I know what Jim is saying, and what in fact he's thinking: that with a knife to his throat, this council member is an enemy. But I don't want to just do it to someone who might be innocent. I push the knife into the man's skin, only an ounce of pressure away from breaking his skin.

The man sweats, his eyes staring at the knife.

"Well?" I ask.

"People are coming," Jim says. "Do it, or forget this whole thing."

Do I have time to think about this? Don't be silly. You know what you have to do, for MacGee and yourself. And Jim won't do anything if he knows you're hesitating.

I push the knife and turn the man's neck away from me. His body flinches, then freezes. His eyes roll back into his head as blood spurts out.

"Let's go," I say wiping the knife on my pants.

After we walk a few buildings over, I stop.

"Get the other men," I say. "Have them take out as many of John's true soldiers as possible. You too. One by one, or more if necessary. But do it without too much hoopla. Then the ones who seem to be on the fence. Bring them to the main hall. Got it?"

Jim's face twitches, then he nods.

I can't have him losing faith. "Remember Mitt and Craig. You want them to have died for nothing?"

"No," he answers, his voice grating and low.

I pat his shoulder and head over to John's building. On the way there, I take a second to tuck my handgun where I can reach it. And in a moment of inspiration, I decide to stuff the knife next to my crotch. It's an uncomfortable walk, but I figure I need to hide it as well as possible. Only once do I stop: when the blade slices a piece of my scrotum and wet blood runs down my leg.

There are three guards outside. I recognize one of them from before.

He raises his hand. "Sorry, John said absolutely no visitors."

"He said he wanted to talk to me," I say, trying to act annoyed. "Don't waste my damn time."

The guard thinks for a moment.

"Is he meeting with someone?" I ask.

"No. But he needs some time alone."

"Well I need to talk to him about the mole. You do understand that Satan is working to cut us all down? Are you going to help him?" This line of talk seems to push them back some, but they're still in front of the door.

"Sorry. He said not even you were to be allowed in."

"Do you think he doesn't want to know who amongst us is trying to tear down His Kingdom?" This too doesn't seem to work. I need to get inside before the fire starts. Once that gets going, I'll be toast.

"Sir—"

"Don't you play games with me," I say. "Let me tell him what's going on through the door."

They step aside. I pound on the door.

"John. Can you hear me? I've got an idea on who's the one working against us. John?"

I hear the shuffling of footsteps. "John?" I ask one more time.

"Let him in," John's voice booms. "Search him first."

His voice crackles, but it's loud. And he's angry. I feel myself shrink, wondering if he knows.

I spread my arms so the men can search me. They pat me down and pull out my handgun. The man searching my legs has yellow eyes. He wraps his hand around my knees. I feel the tension in my head. What will I do if he finds it? Can I take all three men out? The man stops before my crotch area.

"He's clear," he says.

The door opens. I step inside. It's dark, only a few candles are on. I see the outline of John moving to the middle of the room.

"John," I say. "So good to see you." The door closes behind me. I don't like what John's doing. "The children outside were playing in the puddles. It's great to see them have some fun." The smell of soap is stronger than that of dust and rain in here.

"Lock the door," he says.

His tone reminds me of the time I was forced to kneel before him. I do as he says, feeling for the knife that's cutting into the side of my scrotum.

"What was so important, Tom?" he asks.

"I'm sorry, John. Was I disturbing something important?" I half bow my head.

"Don't worry," he says. "I was trying to pray for some guidance."

"I think I know who the mole is. The one working for Lucifer," I say.

"And who's that?" he asks. His interest is hard to gauge.

"Jim. He's trying to round up people to go against you. I heard it from his lips and decided to come here right away."

"Jim?" John says, surprised. "But why?"

"I don't know. I think he's lost his head."

"Jim." John shakes his head.

I take a step towards him. My eyes can see that there's no one else in the room. "What did God say, when you asked him?" I ask. "Did he provide guidance for us? On how to move forward?"

"He was silent," John says, as if that surprised him.

"Is He always like that?"

"Only when He thinks I'm in danger. It's a test. And I've passed them all."

"Of course," I say. "You are chosen by Him."

That seems to make him think. "I am."

"This happen before?"

"Many times. Other council members who thought that they could overpower the will of God. And they all failed, Tom. They all failed."

183

"As anyone who goes up against God must," I say. My heart is bouncing around my body, smashing into muscles. I'm not sure I can stand straight for long, yet alone pull out the knife and do the deed. And his words, booming from that chest of his, are a hand on my body. Freezing me in place. I try to think of Jenny or MacGee, but they're gone. It's me and John.

"They must," John says.

A candle flickers off his eyes. They seem soft, kind. Perhaps it's the idea that he has stopped so many other attempts on his life that's giving me pause. But I have no time. There will be screams once the fire starts. I need to stop John before then. Why is energy leaving my body when I need it most?

"I can't believe it's Jim," John says. "I was hoping that those shafts of light meant some golden times were ahead of us," he says.

And it growls inside me. "They will come," I say. "Let's pray for them. Then we can deal with Jim." I place my hand on his shoulder.

He kneels, and I do too. It's hard to tell if they're truly closed, because the flame dances behind him, shadowing his face. I close my eyes. I can hear his movements: his gentle sways. He murmurs the Lord's Prayer and I do too. When we're done: Amen.

"John," I say, placing a hand on the back of his neck and bringing him close to whisper into his ear. "I'm so thankful for you. You know that?"

John nods.

My other hand reaches slowly down to my pants. I pull the knife up.

"I think we couldn't have a better leader to take us out of the valley of death. You know that?" I say. My hand pulls the handle. Sweat drips. The handle slides out of my hand. I grip it again. The blade nicks the bottom of my shaft, as the handle's stuck in my belt. I gently massage John's neck. "This is what will make us stronger. I'm sure that if we pray on, He will give us guidance." And my hand is out of my pants, with the knife in tow.

"Fire!" A scream goes up. Then a chorus of screams.

John jerks back.

I slash the knife up and at his neck, while bringing his face forward with my other hand.

John's arm blocks mine.

The knife flies out of my hands, and I hear it fall to the ground. How was he so quick? But I can't answer the question as I feel his forehead slam into the bridge of my nose. My eyes water, and I fall backwards, hands in the air. A whining noise makes itself clear in my head.

My back hits the floor. I attempt to stand up. But a kick to my gut knocks the air out of my lungs. I gasp, curling forward, holding my stomach. My body feels paralyzed.

"Did you really think I didn't know, Tom?"

I see his feet.

Another kick to my face sends me flying to the side. I can hear the screams outside. Shots are fired.

"Huh? You think I haven't killed men like you before? Men who thought they could outwit me?" John says. He laughs. The screams outside seem to be subsiding. "What do you have going on out there? Old man Jim helping you?"

Spit lands on my face. I tighten my muscles, waiting for the next kick. John reaches back and swings a leg at me. I collapse my body around his foot and twist it as hard as I can. A cracking sound echoes off the walls. He flies to the ground. As his shadow moves, I see the knife.

I use his leg to leverage my self up. One hand lands on his groin, and I punch his balls as hard as I can. He gasps. His arms reach out to me. Using my body weight, I push them aside and slam my head into his nose. I miss and hit his chin instead. The crack I hear is still satisfying.

I grab his neck, reaching for the knife with my other hand. He's kicking. One hits my side, but I ignore it. The knife is in my hand.

He grabs my neck. Somehow he leverages himself and manages to turn away from me. He's half up now, and my back's on the ground. He falls back on me, knocking my head against the ground. He grabs my mouth with one hand, and my knife-wielding arm with the other.

His strength surprises me. I bite as hard as I can. He screams and pulls his bloody hand away. I use that to kick his leg and throw him off balance. I can taste blood in my mouth. His back's to me. An elbow comes at my face. I turn and it hits me in my neck. My head snaps one way. But I have a hand around his neck. He pulls at that hand. My knife comes at his neck from the other side.

He jerks and reaches for the knife. I'm pushing hard into something, I'm not sure what. It has all the give and push of flesh and ligaments. Warm liquid pours on my hand.

I feel his hand around the knife. I punch him with my other hand on his temple. His entire body is thrashing now. His hand pushes my knife away. I jerk it back. Using jagged slicing movements. I feel his hand loosen its grip on the knife. I slash harder. My other hand still punches him. His head goes limp, dangles to the side.

I pull the knife back. His head is in my lap. I feel like vomiting. Outside the screams seem to have subsided. I get up and stumble around. Every breath I take, it's like I'm breathing in John's soul. I vomit onto the map. Bile and chunks cover the red circles.

This was all for MacGee, I remind myself. Yet I don't feel cleansed. Nor do I even have an inkling of MacGee's forgiveness. Or his joy at me having avenged him. All I know is I feel sick as I look at John's body.

Please. Don't. The words echo in my mind. But they aren't as clear as they once were. In fact, right now, as the warm blood turns my clothes cold, I can't think of a single good reason for this. I stare at the bloody knife, my soaked clothes. I grab a candle and walk over to John's body.

I pat him down to see if he has any weapons. I feel a certain exhaustion, but I know that there's still so much more to do. I need to get by the guards. Spine is all that attaches John's body to his head. It sickens me, then dulls me. I try to just notice the organic material and not think about the man who might have befriended me. Better to lay this on the step of MacGee's death, that moment I had to kiss John's hand, what he said when he kicked me to the ground.

There's nothing on him. And there're no more sounds from outside. People are waiting. You're what's needed out there. And yet I would rather curl up next to John's body and sleep. Maybe cry.

I'm too exhausted for this. What do I say to them? I look up at the ceiling. Am I looking for God's help? After all this, I'm going to look for God's help? My mind shudders. I remember what John told me about the shafts of light. I remember the times I had looked for hope in the land and the nothingness or slaps I received instead.

I take my knife and sever John's head. I grab it by the hair. It's heavy. My mind curls around the idea that the hair is silky. I kick the thought out by staring at the ground. I make sure to keep my eyes away from the head.

I unlock the door and open it. I smell smoke. The guards are looking at me. Their eyes widen, and they step back when they see the head in my hands.

I hold up the knife in my hand. "John was working for the Devil. He asked me to take his life." The certainty with which I speak, scares me. "Are you with me or on the side of the Devil?" They don't answer. "Follow me," I say.

I head over to the main hall. There's no knowing if Jim listened to me. Or whether the burning went successfully. Though I am happy about the silence that seems to pervade the air. Everyone I walk by hugs a wall, recoiling from me. I stare straight ahead. I have no gun. I'm at the mercy of anyone brave enough to shoot me. And yet no one does. Perhaps they never loved John.

Taking the back entrance to the main hall, I step inside. A murmur dies out when people recognize me. I feel the three guards behind me. I wonder what their faces look like. The council is sitting around the main table and one by one they slowly turn to stare at me.

I see where Jim is. He gives me a slight nod. There's something in his eyes that I can't make out. Is it disapproval? Hate? I decide that he too is scared of me.

I give Jim a come here look and he walks over. I feel better. I see the scouts from Thomas' cave standing by the front door.

I place the head on the table. "John's dead. He was working with the Devil. He confessed this in his house. That's something we will have to forever be vigilant for… the Devil amongst us… Is that understood?"

No one says anything. They're all staring at the head.

"I said: is that understood?"

With some reluctance several people nod their heads then mumble their approval. I stare at the council members to see if they have anything to say. They all nod.

"From now on I will be the leader. I have seen the Light of God and I know what He wants. If anyone disagrees, speak now."

Silence. The council members have nothing to say.

"Very well. Let's bow our heads and pray."

I watch as everyone's head bows. I feel warmth rush over me, and a feeling that I was now ready for the future. The Lord's Prayer starts.

THE END

About the Author:

Nelson Lowhim was born in Tanzania where he lived for the first decade of his life. He then lived in India for a year before finally settling in the U.S. in the state of Michigan. He spent some of his formative years hitchhiking and hiking around the great state of Alaska. From there he joined the Army and served for seven years as an Infantryman in 1st AD then as an Engineer in Fifth Group. After his time in the Military—which included many travels through Europe and the Middle East—he came to New York and earned an undergraduate degree from Columbia University. He currently lives with his fiancé in the Bronx.